In Highland Harbors
WITH PARA HANDY

CW00952655

In Highland Harbors
WITH PARA HANDY
NEIL MUNRO

ÆGYPAN PRESS

Special thanks to Jon Jermey.

1911

Neil Munro did much of his best-remembered
work under the pseudonym Hugh Foulis.

In Highland Harbors with Para Handy
A publication of
ÆGYPAN PRESS
www.aegypan.com

Chapter I

NEW COOK

The S.S. *Texa* made a triumphal entry to the harbor by steaming in between two square-rigged schooners, the *Volant* and *Jehu*, of Wick, and slid silently, with the exactitude of long experience, against the piles of Rothesay quay, where Para Handy sat on a log of wood. The throb of her engine, the wash of her propeller, gave place to the strains of a melodeon, which was playing "Stop yer ticklin, Jock," and Para Handy felt some sense of gaiety suffuse him, but business was business, and it was only for a moment he permitted himself to be carried away on the divine wings of music.

"Have you anything for me, M'Kay?" he hailed the *Texa*'s clerk.

The purser cast a rapid glance over the deck, encumbered with planks, crates, casks of paraffin oil, and herring-boxes, and seeing nothing there that looked like a consignment for the questioner, leaned across the rail, and made a rapid survey of the open hold. It held nothing maritime — only hay-bales, flour-bags, soap-boxes, shrouded mutton carcasses, rolls of plumbers' lead, two head-stones for Ardrishaig, and the dismantled slates, cushions, and legs of a billiard-table for Strachur.

"Naething the day for you, Peter," said the clerk; "unless it's yin o' the heid-stanes," and he ran his eye down the manifest which he held in his hand.

"Ye're aawful smert, M'Kay," said Para Handy. "If ye wass a rale purser wi' brass buttons and a yellow-and-black strippit tie on your neck, there would be no haadin' ye in! It's no' luggage I'm lookin' for; it's a kind o' a man I'm expectin'. Maybe he's no' in your department; he'll be traivelin' saloon. Look behind wan o' them herring-boxes, Lachie, and see if ye canna see a sailor."

His intuition was right; the *Texa*'s only passenger that afternoon was discovered sitting behind the herring-boxes playing a melodeon, and smiling beatifically to himself, with blissful unconsciousness that he had arrived at his destination. He came to himself with a start when the purser asked him if he was going off here; terminated the melody of his instrument in a melancholy squawk, picked up a carelessly tied canvas bag that lay at his feet, and hurried over the plank to the quay, shedding from the bag as he went a trail of socks, shoes, collars, penny ballads, and seamen's biscuits, whose exposure in this awkward fashion seemed to cause him no distress of mind, for he only laughed when Para Handy called them to his attention, and left to one of the *Texa's* hands the trouble of collecting them, though he obligingly held the mouth of the sack open himself while the other restored the dunnage. He was a round, short, red-faced, cleanshaven fellow of five-and-twenty, with a thin serge suit, well polished at all the bulgy parts, and a laugh that sprang from a merry heart.

"Are you The Tar's kizzen? Are you Davie Green?" asked Para Handy.

"Right-oh! The very chap," said the stranger. "And you'll be Peter? Haud my melodeon, will ye, till I draw my breath. Right-oh!"

"Are ye sure there's no mistake?" asked Para Handy as they moved along to the other end of the quay where the *Vital Spark* was lying. "You're the new hand I wass expectin', and you name's Davie?"

"My name's Davie, richt enough," said the stranger, "but I seldom got it; when I was on the Cluthas they always ca'd me Sunny Jim."

"Sunny Jum!" said the Captain. "Man! I've often heard aboot ye; you were namely for chumpin' fences?"

"Not me!" said Davie. "Catch me jumpin' onything if there was a hole to get through. Is that your vessel? She's a tipper! You and me'll get on A1. Wait you till ye see the fun I'll gie ye! That was the worst o' the Cluthas — awfu' short trips, and every noo and then a quay; ye hadn't a meenute to yerself for a baur at all. Whit sort o' chaps hae ye for a crew?"

"The very pick!" said Para Handy, as they came alongside the *Vital Spark*, whose crew, as a matter of fact, were all on deck to see the new hand. "That's Macphail, the chief enchineer, wan of Brutain's hardy sons, wi' the wan gallows; and the other chap's Dougie, the first mate, a Cowal laad; you'll see him plainer efter his face iss washed for the tea. Then there's me, mysel', the Captain. Laads, this iss Colin's kizzen, Sunny Jum."

Sunny Jim stood on the edge of the quay, and smiled like a sunset on his future shipmates. "Hoo are yez, chaps?" he cried genially, waving his hand.

"We canna compleen," said Dougie solemnly. "Are ye in good trum yersel'? See's a grup o' your hold-aal, and excuse the gangway."

Sunny Jim jumped on board, throwing his dunnage-bag before him, and his feet had no sooner touched the deck than he indulged in a step or two of the sailor's hornpipe with that proficiency which only years of practice in a close-mouth in Crown Street, S.S., could confer. The Captain looked a little embarrassed; such conduct was hardly businesslike, but it was a relief to find that The Tar's nominee and successor was a cheery chap at any rate. Dougie looked on with no disapproval, but Macphail grunted and turned his gaze to sea, disgusted at such free-and-easy informality.

"I hope ye can cook as weel's ye can dance," he remarked coldly.

Sunny Jim stopped immediately. "Am I supposed to cook?" he asked, concealing his surprise as he best could.

"Ye are that!" said Macphail. "Did ye think ye were to be the German band on board, and go roon' liftin' pennies? Cookin's the main thing wi' the second mate o' the *Vital Spark*, and I can tell ye we're gey particular; are we no', Dougie?"

"Aawful!" said Dougie sadly. "Macphail here hass been cookin' since The Tar left; he'll gie ye his receipt for baddies made wi' enchine-oil."

The *Vital Spark* cast off from Rothesay quay on her way for Bowling, and Sunny Jim was introduced to several pounds of sausages to be fried for dinner, a bag of potatoes, and a jar of salt, with which he was left to juggle as he could, while the others, with expectant appetites, performed their respective duties. Life on the open sea, he found, was likely to be as humdrum as it used to be on the Cluthas, and he determined to initiate a little harmless gaiety. With some difficulty he extracted all the meat from the uncooked sausages, and substituted salt. Then he put them on the frying-pan. They had no sooner heated than they began to dance in the pan with curious little crackling explosions. He started playing his melodeon, and cried on the crew, who hurried to see this unusual phenomenon.

"Well, I'm jeegered," said the Captain; "what in aal the world iss the matter wi' them?"

"It's a waarnin'," said Dougie lugubriously, with wide-staring eyes.

"Warnin', my auntie!" said Sunny Jim, playing a jig-tune. "They started jumpin' like that whenever I begood to play my bonnie wee melodeon."

"I daarsay that," said Para Handy; "for you're a fine, fine player, Jum, but — but it wassna any invitation to a baal I gave them when I paid for them in Ro'sa'."

"I aye said sausages werena meat for sailors," remarked the engineer, with bitterness, for he was very hungry. "Ye'll notice it's an Irish jig they're dancin' to," he added with dark significance.

"I don't see mysel'," said the Captain, "that it maitters whether it iss an Irish jeeg or the Gourock Waltz and Circassian Circle."

"Does it no'?" retorted Macphail. "I suppose ye'll never hae heard o' Irish terrier dugs? I've ett my last sausage onywye! Sling us ower that pan-loaf," and seizing the bread for himself he proceeded to make a spartan meal.

Sunny Jim laughed till the tears ran down his jovial countenance. "Chaps," he exclaimed, with firm conviction, "this is the cheeriest ship ever I was on; I'm awful gled I brung my music."

Dougie took a fork and gingerly investigated. "As hard ass whun-stanes!" he proclaimed; "they'll no' be ready by the time we're at the Tail o' the Bank. Did you ever in your mortal life see the like of it?" and he jabbed ferociously with the fork at the bewitched sausages.

"That's richt!" said Macphail. "Put them oot o' pain."

"Stop you!" said Para Handy. "Let us pause and consuder. It iss the first time ever I saw sassages with such a desperate fine ear for music. If they'll no' fry, they'll maybe boil. Put them in a pot, Jum."

"Right-oh!" said Sunny Jim, delighted at the prospect of a second scene to his farce, and the terpsichorean sausages were consigned to the pot of water which had boiled the potatoes. The crew sat round, staving off the acuter pangs of hunger with potatoes and bread.

"You never told us what for they called you Sunny Jum, Davie," remarked the Captain. "Do you think it would be for your complexion?"

"I couldna say," replied the new hand, "but I think mysel' it was because I was aye such a cheery wee chap. The favorite Clutha on the Clyde, when the Cluthas was rinnin', was the yin I was on; hunners o' trips used to come wi' her on the Setturdays on the aff-chance that I wad maybe gie them a baur. Mony a pant we had! I could hae got a job at the Finnieston Ferry richt enough, chaps, but they wouldna alloo the melodeon, and I wad sooner want my wages."

"A fine, fine unstrument!" said Para Handy agreeably. "Wi' it and Dougie's trump we'll no' be slack in passin' the time."

"Be happy! — that's my motto," said Sunny Jim, beaming upon his auditors like one who brings a new and glorious evangel. "Whatever happens, be happy, and then ye can defy onything. It's a' in the wye ye look at things. See?"

"That's what I aalways say mysel' to the wife," said Dougie in heart-broken tones, and his eye on the pot, which was beginning to boil briskly.

"As shair as daith, chaps, I canna stand the Jock o' Hazeldean kind o' thing at a' — folk gaun aboot lettin' the tear doon-fa a' the time. Gie me a hearty laugh and it's right-oh! *Be happy!* — that's the Golden Text for the day, as we used to say in the Sunday School."

"I could be happy easy enough if it wassna that I wass so desperate hungry," said Dougie in melancholy accents, lifting the lid to look into the pot. He could see no sign of sausages, and with new forebodings he began to feel for them with a stick. They had disappeared! "I said from the very first it wass a waamin'!" he exclaimed, resigning the stick to the incredulous engineer.

"This boat's haunted," said Macphail, who also failed to find anything in the pot. "I saw ye puttin' them in wi' my ain eyes, and noo they're no' there."

Para Handy grabbed the spirtle, and feverishly explored on his own account, with the same extraordinary results.

"My Chove!" he exclaimed, "did you ever see the like of that, and I havena tasted wan drop of stimulants since last Monday. Laads! I don't know what you think aboot it, but it's the church twice for me tomorrow!"

Sunny Jim quite justified his nickname by giving a pleasant surprise to his shipmates in the shape of a meat-tea later in the afternoon.

Chapter II

PENSION FARMS

*T*he *Vital Spark* was making for Lochgoilhead, Dougie at the wheel, and the Captain straddled on a water-breaker, humming Gaelic songs, because he felt magnificent after his weekly shave. The chug-chug-chug of the engines was the only other sound that broke the silence of the afternoon, and Sunny Jim deplored the fact that in the hurry of embarking early in the morning he had quite forgotten his melodeon — those peaceful days at sea hung heavy on his urban spirit.

"That's Ardgoil," remarked Macphail, pointing with the stroup of an oil-can at the Glasgow promontory, and Para Handy gazed at the land with affected interest.

"So it iss, Macphail," he said ironically. "That wass it the last time we were here, and the time before, and the time before that again. You would think it would be shifted. It's wan of them guides for towerists you should be, Macphail, you're such a splendid hand for information. What way do you spell it?"

"Oh, shut up!" said the engineer with petulance; "ye think ye're awfu' clever. I mind when that wee hoose at the p'int was a hen farm, and there's no' a road to't. Ye could only get near the place wi' a boat."

"If that wass the way of it," said Dougie, "ducks would suit them better; they could swim. It's a fine thing a duck."

"But a goose is more extraordinar'," said Macphail with meaning. "Anyway it was hens, and mony a time I wished I had a ferm for hens."

"You're better where you are," said the Captain, "oilin' engines like a chentleman. A hen ferm iss an aawful speculation, and you need your wuts aboot you if you start wan. All your relations expect their eggs for nothing, and the very time o' the year when eggs iss dearest, hens takes a tirrievee and stop the layin'. Am I no' tellin' the truth, Dougie?"

"You are that!" said the mate agreeably; "I have noticed it mysel'."

"If ye didna get eggs ye could live aff the chickens," suggested Sunny Jim. "I think a hen ferm would be top, richt enough!"

"It's not the kind o' ferm I would have mysel' whatever o't," said Para Handy; "there's far more chance o' a dacent livin' oot o' rearin' pensioners."

"Rearin' pensioners?" remarked Macphail; "ye would lie oot o' your money a lang while rearin' pensioners; ye micht as weel start growin' trees."

"Not at aal! not at aal!" said Para Handy; "there's quick returns in pensioners if you put your mind to the thing and use a little caation. Up in the Islands, now, the folks iss givin' up their crofts and makin' a kind o' ferm o' their aged relations. I have a cousin yonder oot in Gigha wi' a stock o' five fine healthy uncles — no' a man o' them under seventy. There's another frien' o' my own in Mull wi' thirteen heid o' chenuine old Macleans. He gaitbered them aboot the islands wi' a boat whenever the rumors o' the pensions started. Their frien's had no idea what he wanted wi' them, and were glad to get them off their hands. 'It's chust a notion that I took,' he said, 'for company; they're great amusement on a winter night,' and he got his pick o' the best o' them. It wassna every wan he would take; they must be aal Macleans, for the Mull Macleans never die till they're centurions, and he wouldna take a man that wass over five and seventy. They're yonder, noo, in Loch Scridain, kept like fightin' cocks; he puts them oot on the hill each day for exercise, and if wan o' them takes a cough they dry his clothes and give him something from a bottle."

"Holy smoke!" said Dougie; "where's the profits comin' from?"

"From the Government," said Para Handy. "Nothing simpler! He gets five shillings a heid in the week for them, and that's £169 in the year for the whole thirteen — enough to feed a regiment! Wan pensioner maybe wadna pay you, but if you have a herd like my frien' in Mull, there's money in it. He buys their meal in bulk from Oban, and they'll grow their own potatoes; the only thing he's vexed for iss that they havena wool, and he canna clip them. If he keeps his health himsel', and doesna lose his heid for a year or twa, he'll have the lergest pension ferm in Scotland, and be able to keep a gig. I'm no' a bit feared for Donald, though; he's a man o' business chust ass good ass you'll get on the streets o' Gleska."

"Thirteen auld chaps like that aboot a noose wad be an awfu' handful," suggested Sunny Jim.

"Not if it's at Loch Scridain," answered Para Handy; "half the time they're on the gress, and there's any amount o' fanks. They're quite delighted swappin' baurs wi' wan another aboot the way they could throw the hammer fifty years ago, and they feel they're more important noo than ever they were in a' their lives afore. When my frien' collected them, they hadna what you would caal an object for to live for except it wass their own funerals; noo they're daft for almanacs, and makin' plans for living to a hundred, when the former tells them that he'll gie them each a medal and a uniform. Oh! a smert, smert laad, Donal'. Wan o'Brutain's hardy sons! Nobody could be kinder!"

"It's a fine way o' makin' a livin'," said Macphail. "I hope they'll no' go wrang wi' him."

"Fine enough," said Para Handy, "but the chob iss not withoot responsibilities. Yonder's my cousin in Gigha wi' his stock o' five, and a nice bit ground for them, and you wouldna believe what it needs in management. He got two of them pretty cheap in Salen, wan o' them over ninety, and the other eighty-six; you wouldna believe it, but they're worse to manage than the other three that's ten years younger. The wan over ninety's very cocky of his age, and thinks the other wans iss chust a lot o' boys. He says it's a scandal givin' them a pension; pensions should be kept for men that's up in years, and then it should be something sensible — something like a pound. The wan that iss eighty-six iss desperate dour, and if my cousin doesna please him, stays in his bed and says he'll die for spite."

"That's gey mean, richt enough!" said Sunny Jim; "efter your kizzen takin' a' that trouble!"

"But the worst o' the lot's an uncle that he got in Eigg; he's seventy-six, and talkin' aboot a wife!"

"Holy smoke!" said Dougie; "isn't that chust desperate!"

"Aye; he hass a terrible conceity notion o' his five shillin's a-week; you would think he wass a millionaire. 'I could keep a wife on it if she wass young and strong,' he tells my cousin, and it takes my cousin and the mustress aal their time to keep him oot o' the way o' likely girls. They don't ken the day they'll lose him."

"Could they no' put a brand on him?" asked Dougie.

"Ye daurna brand them," said the Captain, "nor keel them either. The law'll not allo' it. So you see yersel's there's aye a risk, and it needs a little capital. My cousin had a bit of a shop, and he gave it up to start the pension term; he'll be sayin' sometimes it wass a happier man he wass when he wass a merchant, but he's awfu' prood that noo he hass a chob, as you might say, wi' the Brutish Government."

Chapter III

PARA HANDY'S PUP

One night when the *Vital Spark* lay at Port Ellen quay, and all the crew were up the village at a shinty concert, someone got on board the vessel and stole her best chronometer. It was the property of Macphail, had cost-exactly 1s. 11d., and kept approximate time for hours on end if laid upon its side. Macphail at frequent intervals repaired it with pieces of lemonade wire, the selvedges of postage stamps, and a tube of seccotine.

"Holy smoke!" said the Captain, when the loss was discovered; "we'll be sleepin' in in the efternoons as sure as anything. Isn't this the depredation!"

"The champion wee nock!" said Macphail, on the verge of tears. "Set it to the time fornenst yon nock o' Singersers at Kilbowie, and it would tick as nate as onything to the Cloch."

"Right enough!" said Sunny Jim impressively;

"I've biled eggs wi't. There's the very nail it hung on!"

"It's the first time I ever knew that nock to go without Macphail doin' something to it wi' the stroup o' an oil-can," said Dougie.

It was decided that no more risks of quay-head burglary were to be run, and that when evening entertainments called the rest of the crew ashore, the charge of the ship should depend on Sunny Jim.

"I couldna tak' it in haund, chaps!" he protested feelingly. "Ye've nae idea hoo silly I am at nicht when I'm my lane; I cod mysel' I'm seein' ghosts till every hair on my heid's on end."

"I'm like that mysel'!" confessed Para Handy. "I can gie mysel' a duvvle o' a fright, but it's only nonsense, chust fair nonsense!

there's no' a ghost this side o' the Sound o' Sleat; nothing but imagination."

"Ye shouldna be tumid!" counseled Dougie, who never could stay in the fo'c'sle alone at night himself for fear of spirits.

"Ye'll can play your melodeon," said Macphail; "if there's onything to scare the life oot o' ghosts it's that."

But Sunny Jim was not to be induced to run the risk, and the Captain wasn't the sort of man to compel a body to do a thing he didn't like to do, against his will. Evening entertainments at the ports of call were on the point of being regretfully foresworn, when Sunny Jim proposed the purchase of a watchdog. "A watch-dug's the very ticket," he exclaimed. "It's an awfu' cheery thing on a boat. We can gie't the rin o' the deck when we're ashore at nicht, and naebody'll come near't. I ken the very dug — it belangs to a chap in Fairfield, a rale Pompanion, and he ca's it Biler. It has a pedigree and a brass-mounted collar, and a' its P's and Q's."

"Faith! there's worse things than a good dog; there's some o' them chust sublime!" said Para Handy, quite enamored of the notion. "Iss it well trained, your frien's Pompanion?"

"Top!" Sunny Jim assured him. "If ye jist seen it! It would face a regiment o' sodgers, and has a bark ye could hear from here to Campbeltown. It's no awfu' fancy-lookin', mind; it's no' the kind ye'll see the women carryin' doon Buchanan Street in their oxters; but if ye want sagaciosity — !" and Sunny Jim held up his hands in speechless admiration of the animal's intelligence. "It belangs to a riveter ca'd Willie Stevenson, and it's jist a pup. There's only the wan fau't wi't, or Willie could live aff the prizes it wad lift at shows — it's deaf."

"That's the very sort o' dug we wad need for a boat like this," said Macphail, with his usual cynicism. "Could ye no' get yin that was blin' too?" But nobody paid any attention to him; there were moments when silent contempt was the obvious attitude to the engineer.

"The worst about a fine, fine dog like that," said Para Handy reflectively, "iss that it would cost a lot o' money, and aal we want iss a dog to watch the boat and bark daily or hourly ass required."

"Cost!" retorted Sunny Jim; "it wad cost nae-thing! I wad ask Willie Stevenson for the len' o't, and then say we lost it ower the side. It has far mair sense than Willie himsel'. It goes aboot Govan wi' him on pay Setturdays, and sleeps between his feet when he's sittin' in the public-hooses backin' up the Celts. Sometimes Willie forget's it's wi' him, and gangs awa' without waukenin' 't, but when Biler waukens up and sees its maister's no there, it stands on its hind legs and looks at the gless that Willie was drinkin' frae. If there's ony drink left in't it kens he'll be back, and it waits for him."

"Capital!" said Para Handy. "There's dogs like that. It's born in them. It's chust a gift!"

The dog Biler was duly borrowed by Sunny Jim on the next run to Glasgow, and formally installed as watch of the *Vital Spark*. It was distinctly not the sort of dog to make a lady's pet; its lines were generously large, but crude and erratic; its coat was hopelessly unkempt and ragged, its head incredibly massive, and its face undeniably villainous. Even Sunny Jim was apologetic when he produced it on a chain. "Mind, I never said he was onything awfu' fancy," he pleaded. "But he's a dug that grows on ye."

"He's no' like what I thocht he would be like at aal, at aal," admitted the Captain, somewhat disappointed. "Iss he a rale Pompanion?"

"Pure bred!" said Sunny Jim; "never lets go the grip. Examine his jaw."

"Look you at his jaw, Dougie, and see if he's the rale Pompanion," said the Captain; but Dougie declined. "I'll wait till we're better acquent," he said. "Man! doesn't he look desperate dour?"

"Oor new nock's a' right wi' a dug like that to watch it," said Macphail; "he's as guid as a guardship."

Biler surveyed them curiously, not very favorably impressed, and deaf, of course, to all blandishments. For a day or two the slightest hasty movement on the part of any of his new companions made him growl ferociously and display an appalling arsenal of teeth. As a watchdog he was perfect; nobody dared come down a quay within a hundred yards of the *Vital Spark* without his loud, alarming bay. Biler spoiled the quay-head angling all along Loch Fyne.

In a week or two Para Handy got to love him, and bragged incessantly of his remarkable intelligence. "Chust a pup!" he would say, "but as long in the heid as a weedow woman. If he had aal his faculties he would not be canny, and indeed he doesna seem to want his hearin' much; he's ass sharp in the eye ass a polisman. A dog like that should have a Board of Tred certuficate."

Dougie, however, was always dubious of the pet. "Take my word, Peter," he would say solemnly, "there's muschief in him; he's no a dog you can take to your he'rt at aal, at aal, and he barks himsel' black in the face wi' animosity at Macphail."

"Didn't I tell you?" would the Captain cry, exultant. "Ass deaf ass a door, and still he can take the measure o' Macphail! I hope, Jum, your frien' in Fairfield's no' in a hurry to get him back."

"Not him," said Sunny Jim. "He's no expectin' him back at a'. I tell't him Biler was drooned at Colintraive, and a' he said was 'ye micht hae tried to save his collar.'"

And Dougie's doubts were fully justified in course of time. The *Vital Spark* was up with coals at Skipness, at a pier a mile away from the village, and Para Handy had an invitation to a party. He dressed himself in his Sunday clothes, and, redolent of scented soap, was confessed the lion of the evening, though Biler unaccountably refused to accompany him. At midnight he came back along the shore, to the ship, walking airily on his heels, with his hat at a dashing angle. The crew of the *Vital Spark* were all asleep, but the faithful Biler held the deck, and the Captain heard his bark.

"Pure Pompanion bred!" he said to himself. "As wise as a weedow woman! For the rale sagacity give me a dog!"

He made to step from the quay to the vessel's gunnel, but a rush and a growl from the dog restrained him; Biler's celebrated grip was almost on his leg.

"Tuts, man," said the Captain, "I'm sure you can see it's me; it's Peter. Good old Biler; stop you and I'll give you a buscuit!"

He ventured a foot on the gunnel again, and this time Biler sampled the tweed of his trousers. Nothing else was stirring in the *Vital Spark*. The Captain hailed his shipmates for assistance; if they heard, they never heeded, and the situation was sufficiently unpleasant to annoy a man of better temper even than Para Handy. No matter how he tried to get on board, the trusty watchdog kept him back. In one attempt his hat fell off, and Biler tore it into the most impressive fragments.

"My Cot," said the Captain, "issn't this the happy evenin'? Stop you till I'll be pickin' a dog again, and it'll be wan wi' aal his faculties."

He had to walk back to the village and take shelter ashore for the night; in the morning Biler received him with the friendliest overtures, and was apparently astonished at the way they were received.

"Jum," said the Captain firmly, "you'll take back that dog to your frien' in Fairfield, and tell him there's no' a bit o' the rale Pompanion in him. He's chust a common Gleska dog, and he doesna know a skipper when he sees him, if he's in his Sunday clothes."

Chapter IV

TREASURE TROVE

Sunny Jim proved a most valuable acquisition to the *Vital Spark*. He was a person of humor and resource, and though they were sometimes the victims of his practical jokes, the others of the crew forgave him readily because of the fun he made. It is true that when they were getting the greatest entertainment from him they were, without thinking it, generally doing his work for him — for indeed he was no sailor, only a Clutha mariner — but at least he was better value for his wages than The Tar, who could neither take his fair share of the work nor tell a baur. Sunny Jim's finest gift was imagination; the most wonderful things in the world had happened to him when he was on the Cluthas — all intensely interesting, if incredible: and Para Handy, looking at him with admiration and even envy, after a narrative more extraordinary than usual, would remark, "Man! it's a peety listenin' to such d — d lies iss a sin, for there iss no doobt it iss a most pleasant amuusement!"

Macphail the engineer, the misanthrope, could not stand the new hand. "He's no' a sailor at a'!" he protested; "he's a clown; I've see'd better men jumpin' through girrs at a penny show."

"Weel, he's maybe no' aawful steady at the wheel, but he hass a kyind, kyind he'rt!" Dougie said.

"He's chust sublime!" said Para Handy. "If he wass managed right there would be money in him!"

Para Handy's conviction that there was money to be made out of Sunny Jim was confirmed by an episode at Tobermory, of which the memory will be redolent in Mull for years to come.

The *Vital Spark*, having discharged a cargo of coal at Oban, went up the Sound to load with timber, and on Calve Island, which forms a natural breakwater for Tobermory harbor, Dougie spied a stranded whale. He was not very much of a whale as whales go in

Greenland, being merely a tiny fellow of about five-and-twenty tons, but as dead whales here are as rarely to be seen as dead donkeys, the *Vital Spark* was steered close in to afford a better view, and even stopped for a while that Para Handy and his mate might land with the punt on the islet and examine the unfortunate cetacean.

"My Chove! he's a whupper!" was Dougie's comment, as he reached up and clapped the huge mountain of sea-flesh on its ponderous side. "It wass right enough, I can see, Peter, aboot yon fellow Jonah; chust look at the accommodation!"

"Chust waste, pure waste," said the skipper; "you can make a meal off a herein', but whales iss only lumber, goin' aboot ass big as a land o' hooses, blowin' aal the time, and puttin' the fear o' daith on aal the other fushes. I never had mich respect for them."

"If they had a whale like that aground on Clyde," said Dougie, as they returned to the vessel, "they would stick bills on't; it's chust thrown away on the Tobermory folk."

Sunny Jim was enchanted when he heard the whale's dimensions. "Chaps," he said with enthusiasm, "there's a fortune in't; right-oh! I've see'd them chargin' tuppence to get into a tent at Vinegar Hill, whaur they had naethin' fancier nor a sea-lion or a seal."

"But they wouldna be deid," said Para Handy; "and there's no' mich fun aboot a whale's remains. Even if there was, we couldna tow him up to Gleska, and if we could, he wouldna keep."

"Jim'll be goin' to embalm him, rig up a mast on him, and sail him up the river; are ye no', Jim?" said Macphail with irony.

"I've a faur better idea than that," said Sunny Jim. "Whit's to hinder us clappin' them tarpaulins roon' the whale whaur it's lyin', and showin' 't at a sixpence a heid to the Tobermory folk? Man! ye'll see them rowin' across in hunners, for I'll bate ye there's no much fun in Tobermory in the summertime unless it's a Band o' Hope soiree. Give it a fancy name – the 'Tobermory Treasure'; send the bellman roond the toon, sayin' it's on view tomorrow from ten till five, and then goin' on to Oban; Dougie'll lift the money, and the skipper and me'll tell the audience a' aboot the customs o' the whale when he's in life. Macphail can stand by the ship at Tobermory quay."

"Jist what I said a' alang," remarked Macphail darkly. "Jumpin' through girrs! Ye'll need a big drum and a naphtha lamp."

"Let us first paause and consider," remarked Para Handy, with his usual caution; "iss the whale oors?"

"Wha's else wad it be?" retorted Sunny Jim. "It was us that fun' it, and naebody seen it afore us, for it's no' mony oors ashore."

"Everything cast up on the shore belangs to the Crown; it's the King's whale," said Macphail.

"Weel, let him come for't," said Sunny Jim; "by the time he's here we'll be done wi't."

The presumption that Tobermory could be interested in a dead whale proved quite right; it was the Glasgow Fair week, and the local boat-hirers did good business taking parties over to the island where an improvised enclosure of oars, spars, and tarpaulin and dry sails concealed the "Tobermory Treasure" from all but those who were prepared to pay for admission. Para Handy, with his hands in his pockets and a studied air of indifference, as if the enterprise was none of his, chimed in at intervals with facts in the natural history of the whale, which Sunny Jim might overlook in the course of his introductory lecture.

"The biggest whale by three feet that's ever been seen in Scotland," Sunny Jim announced. "Lots o' folk thinks a whale's a fish, but it's naething o' the kind; it's a hot-blooded mammoth, and couldna live in the waiter mair nor a wee while at a time withoot comin' up to draw its breath. This is no' yin of thae common whales that chases herrin', and goes pechin' up and doon Kilbrannan Sound; it's the kind that's catched wi' the harpoons and lives on naething but roary borealises and icebergs."

"They used to make umbrella-rubs wi' this parteecular kind," chimed in the skipper diffidently; "forbye, they're full o' blubber. It's an aawful useful thing a whale, chentlemen." He had apparently changed his mind about the animal, for which the previous day he had said he had no respect.

"Be shair and tell a' your friends when ye get ashore that it's maybe gaun on to Oban tomorrow," requested Sunny Jim. "We'll hae it up on the Esplanade there and chairge a shillin' a heid; if we get it the length o' Gleska, the price'll be up to hauf-a-croon."

"Is it a 'right' whale?" asked one of the audience in the interests of exact science.

"Right enough, as shair's onything; isn't it. Captain?" said Sunny Jim.

"What else would it be?" said Para Handy indignantly. "Does the chentleman think there iss onything wrong with it? Perhaps he would like to take a look through it; eh, Jum? Or maybe he would want a doctor's certeeficate that it's no a dromedary."

The exhibition of the "Tobermory Treasure" proved so popular that its discoverers determined to run their entertainment for about a week. On the third day passengers coming into Tobermory with the steamer Claymore sniffed with appreciation, and talked about the beneficial influence of ozone; the English tourists debated whether it was due to peat or heather. In the afternoon several yachts in the bay hurriedly got up their anchors and went up Loch Sunart, where the air seemed fresher. On the fourth day the residents of Tobermory overwhelmed the local chemist with demands for camphor, carbolic powder, permanganate of potash, and other deodorants and disinfectants; and several plumbers were telegraphed for to Oban. The public patronage of the exhibition on Calve Island fell off.

"If there's ony mair o' them wantin' to see this whale," said Sunny Jim, "they'll hae to look slippy."

"It's no' that bad to windward," said Para Handy. "What would you say to coverin' it up wi' more tarpaulins?"

"You might as weel cover't up wi' crape or muslin," was Dougie's verdict. "What you would need iss armor-plate, the same ass they have roond the cannons in the man-o'-wars. If this wind doesn't change to the west, half the folk in Tobermory 'll be goin' to live in the cellar o' the Mishnish Hotel."

Suspicion fell on the "Tobermory Treasure" on the following day, and an influential deputation waited on the police sergeant, while the crew of the *Vital Spark*, with much discretion, abandoned their whale, and kept to their vessel's fo'c'sle. The sergeant informed the deputation that he had a valuable clue to the source of these extraordinary odors, but that unfortunately he could take no steps without a warrant from the Sheriff, and the Sheriff was in Oban. The deputation pointed out that the circumstances were too serious to permit of any protracted legal forms and ceremonies; the whale must be removed from Calve Island by its owners immediately, otherwise there would be a plague. With regret the police sergeant repeated that he could do nothing without authority, but he added casually that if the deputation visited the owners of the whale and scared the life out of them, he would be the last man to interfere.

"Hullo, chaps! pull the hatch efter yez, and keep oot the cold air!" said Sunny Jim, as the spokesman of the deputation came seeking for the crew in the fo'o'sle. "Ye'd be the better o' some odecolong on your hankies."

"We thought you were going to remove your whale to Oban before this," said the deputation sadly.

"I'm afraid," said Para Handy, "that whale hass seen its best days, and wouldna be at aal popular in Oban."

"Well, you'll have to take it out of here immediately anyway," said the deputation. "It appears to be your property."

"Not at aal, not at aal!" Para Handy assured him; "it belongs by right to His Majesty, and we were chust takin' care of it for him till he would turn up, chairgin' a trifle for the use o' the tarpaulins and the management. It iss too great a responsibility now, and we've given up the job; aren't we, Jum?"

"Right-oh!" said Sunny Jim, reaching for his melodeon; "and it's time you Tobermory folk were shiftin' that whale."

"It's impossible," said the deputation, "a carcase weighing nearly thirty tons — and in such a condition!"

"Indeed it is pretty bad," said Para Handy; "perhaps it would be easier to shift the toon o' Tobermory."

But that was, luckily, not necessary, as a high tide restored the "Tobermory Treasure" to its natural element that very afternoon.

Chapter V

LUCK

*P*ara Handy, gossiping with his crew, and speaking generally of "luck" and the rewards of industry and intelligence, always counted luck the strongest agent in the destiny of man. "Since ever I wass a skipper," he said, "I had nobody in my crew that was not lucky; I would sooner have lucky chaps on board wi' me than tip-top sailors that had a great experience o' wrecks. If the *Fital Spark* hass the reputation o' bein' the smertest vessel in the coastin' tred, it's no' aal-thegither wi' navigation; it's chust because I had luck mysel', and aalways had a lot o' lucky laads aboot me. Dougie himsel' 'll tell you that."

"We have plenty o' luck," admitted Dougie, nursing a wounded head he had got that day by carelessly using it as a fender to keep the side of the ship from the piles of Tarbert quay. "We have plenty of luck, but there must be a lot o' cluver people never mindin' mich aboot their luck, and gettin' aal the money."

"Money!" said the Captain with contempt; "there's other things to think aboot than money. If I had as mich money ass I needed, I wouldna ask for a penny more. There's nothing bates content-ment and a pleesant way o' speakin' to the owners. You needna empty aal the jar o' jam, Macphail; give him a rap on the knuckles, Jum, and tak' it from him."

Macphail relinquished the jam-jar readily, because he had fin-ished all that was in it. "If ye had mair luck and less jaw aboot it," said he snappishly, "ye wadna hae to wait so lang on the money ye're expectin' frae your cousin Cherlie in Dunmore. Is he no deid yet?"

"No," said Para Handy dolefully; "he's still hangin' on; I never heard o' a man o' ninety-three so desperate deleeberate aboot dyin', and it the wintertime. Last Friday week wass the fifth time they sent to Tarbert for the munister, and he wasna needed."

"That was your cousin Cherlie's luck," said the engineer, who was not without logic.

"I don't caal that luck at aal," retorted Para Handy; "I call it just manoeuvrin'. Forbye, it wasna very lucky for the munister."

Cousin Cherlie's deliberation terminated a week later, when the *Vital Spark* was in Loch Pyne, and the Captain borrowed a hat and went to the funeral. "My own roond hat iss a good enough hat and quite respectable," he said, "but someway it doesna fit for funerals since I canna wear it on my heid except it's cocked a little to the side. You see, I have been at so many Tarbert Fairs with it, and highjeenks chenerally."

The crew helped to make his toilet. Macphail, with a piece of oily engine-room waste, imparted a resplendent polish to the borrowed hat, which belonged to a Tarbert citizen, and had lost a good deal of its original luster. Dougie contributed a waistcoat, and Sunny Jim cheerfully sacrificed his thumb-nails in fastening the essential, but unaccustomed, collar on his Captain's neck. "There ye are, skipper," he said; "ye look Al if ye only had a clean hanky."

"I'm no feelin' in very good trum, though," said the Captain, who seemed to be almost throttled by the collar; "there's no' mich fun for us sailor chaps in bein' chentlemen. But of course it's no' every day we're buryin' Cherlie, and I'm his only cousin, no' coontin' them MacNeills."

"Hoo much did ye say he had?" asked Macphail. "Was it a hunder pounds and a free hoose? or a hunder free hooses and a pound?"

"Do you know, laads," said the Captain, "his money wasna in my mind!"

"That's wi' the ticht collar," said the engineer unfeelingly; "lowse yer collar and mak' up yer mind whit yer gaun to dae wi' the hunder pounds. That's to say, if the MacNeills don't get it."

The Captain's heart, at the very thought of such disaster, came to his throat, and burst the fastenings of his collar, which had to be rigged up anew by Sunny Jim.

"The MacNeills," he said, "'ll no' touch a penny. Cherlie couldna stand them, and I wass aye his favorite, me bein' a captain. Money would be wasted on the MacNeills; they wouldna know what to do wi't."

"I ken whit I wad dae wi' a hunder pound if I had it," said Macphail emphatically.

"You would likely gie up the sea and retire to the free hoose wi' a ton or two o' your penny novelles," suggested the Captain.

"I wad trevel," said the engineer, heedless of the unpleasant innuendo. "There's naething like trevel for widenin' the mind. When I was sailin' foreign I saw a lot o' life, but I didna see near sae much as I wad hae seen if I had the money."

"Fancy a sailor traivellin'!" remarked Sunny Jim. "There's no much fun in that."

"I don't mean traivellin' in boats," explained Macphail. "Ye never see onything trevellin' in boats; I mean trains. The only places abroad worth seein' 's no' to be seen at the heid o' a quay; ye must tak' a train to them. Rome, and Paris, and the Eyetalian Lakes — that sort o' thing. Ye live in hotels and any amount o' men's ready to carry yer bag. Wi' a hunder pound a man could trevel the world."

"Never heed him, Peter," said Dougie; "trevellin's an anxious business; you're aye losin' your tickets, and the tips you have to give folk's a fair ruination. If I had a hunder pound and a free hoose, I would let the hoose and tak' a ferm."

"A ferm's no' bad," admitted Para Handy, "but there's a desperate lot o' work aboot a ferm."

"There's a desperate lot o' work aboot anything ye can put your hand to, except enchineerin'," said Dougie sadly, "but you can do wonders if you have a good horse and a fine strong wife. You wouldna need to be a rale former, but chust wan o' them chentleman termers that wears knickerbockers and yellow leggin's."

"There's a good dale in what you say," Dougie, admitted the Captain, who saw a pleasing vision of himself in yellow leggings. "It's no' a bad tred, chentleman fermin'."

"Tred!" said Dougie; "it's no a tred — it's a recreation, like sailin' a yat. Plooin'-matches and 'ool-markets every other day; your own eggs and all the mutton and milk you need for nothing. Buy you a ferm, Peter, I'm tellin' you!"

"Chust that!" said the Captain cunningly. "And then maybe you would be skipper of the *Fital Spark,* Dougie."

"I wasna thinkin' aboot that at aal!" protested the mate.

"I wasna sayin' you were," said the Captain, "but the mustress would give you the notion."

"If I was you I wad tak' a shop in Gleska," said Sunny Jim. "No' an awfu' big shop, but a handy wee wan ye could shut when there was any sport on withoot mony people noticin'."

Para Handy buttoned his coat, and prepared to set out for the funeral. "Whether it wass trevellin', or a ferm, or a shop, I would get on sublime, for I'm a lucky, lucky man, laads; but I'm no lettin' my mind dwell on Cherlie's money, oot o' respect for my relative. I'll see you aal when I come back, and maybe it might be an Occasion."

Dougie cried after him when he was a little up the quay, "Captain, your hat's chust a little to the side."

Para Handy was back from the funeral much sooner than was expected, his collar in his pocket, and the borrowed hat in his hand. He went below to resume his ordinary habiliments without a word to the crew, who concluded that he was discreetly concealing the legacy. When he came up, they asked no questions, from a sense of proper decorum, but the Captain seemed surcharged with great emotion.

"Dougie," he said to the mate, "what would be the cost o' a pair o' yellow leggin's?"

"Aboot a pound," said the mate, with some exultation. "Have you made up your mind for fermin'?"

"No," said the Captain bitterly; "but I might afford the leggin's off my cousin Cherlie's legacy, but it wouldna go the length o' knickerbockers."

Chapter VI

SALVAGE FOR THE 'VITAL SPARK'

The vessel was rounding Ardlamont in a sou'wester that set her all awash like an empty herring-box. Over her snub nose combed appalling sprays; green seas swept her fore and aft; she was glucking with internal waters, and her squat red funnel whooped dolorously with wind. "Holy smoke!" gasped Para Handy, "isn't this the hammerin'!"

"A sailor's life!" said Dougie bitterly, drawing a soaking sleeve across his nose; "I would sooner be a linen-draper."

In flaws of the wind they could hear Macphail break coals in the engine-room, and the wheezy tones of Sunny Jim's melodeon as he lay on his bunk in the fo'c'sle quelling his apprehensions to the air of "The Good Old Summertime." Together at the wheel the Captain and his mate were dismal objects, drenched to the hide, even below their oil-skins, which gave them the glistening look of walruses or seals. They had rigged a piece of jib up for a dodger; it poorly served its purpose, and seemed as inefficient as a hand-kerchief as they raised their blinking eyes above it and longingly looked for the sheltering arms of the Kyles.

"I wish to the Lord it wass Bowlin' quay and me sound sleepin'," said the mate. "Yonder's the mustress in Plantation snug and cozy on't, and I'll wager she's no' a bit put aboot for her man on the heavin' bullow. It makes me quite angry to think of it. Eggs for her tea and all her orders, and me with not a bite since breakfast-time but biscuits."

"Holy smoke! you surely wouldna like her to be wi' you here," said Para Handy, shocked.

"No," said Dougie, "but I wish she could see me noo, and I wish I could get her and her high tea at the fireside oot on' my heid; it's bad enough to be standing here like a flagpole thinkin' every meenute'll be my next."

"Toot! man, Dougie, you're tumid, tumid," said the Captain. "Draw your braith as deep's you can, throw oot your chest, and be a hero. Look at me! my name's Macfarlane and I'm wan of Brutain's hardy sons!"

The Vital Spurk got round the Point, and met a wave that smashed across her counter and struck full in the face the mariners at the wheel. Dougie, with his mouth inelegantly open, swallowed a pint or two, and spluttered. Para Handy shook the water from his beard like a spaniel, and looking more anxiously than before through smarting eyes, saw a gabbart laboring awkwardly close on the shore of Ettrick Bay.

"Dougie," said he, "stop giggling a bit, and throw your eye to starboard — is yon no' the Katherine Anne?"

"It wassna giggling I wass," said Dougie irritably, coughing brine, "but I nearly spoiled the Kyles o' Bute. It's the Katherine-Anne right enough, and they've lost command o' her; stop you a meenute and you'll hear an awfu' dunt."

"She'll be ashore in a juffy," said the Captain tragically. "Man! iss it no' chust desperate! I'm no' makin' a proposeetion, mind, but what would you say to givin' a slant across and throwin' a bit o' a rope to her?"

Dougie looked wistfully at Tighnabruaich ahead of them, and now to be reached in comfort, and another at the welter of waves between them and the struggling gabbart. "Whatever you say yoursel', Peter," he replied, and for twenty minutes more they risked disaster. At one wild moment Para Handy made his way to the fo'c'sle hatch and bellowed down to Sunny Jim, "You there wi' your melodeon — it would fit you better if you tried to mind your Psalms."

When they reached the Katherine-Anne, and found she had been abandoned. Para Handy cursed at first his own soft heart that had been moved to the distress of a crew who were comfortably on their way to Rothesay. He was for leaving the gabbart to her fate, but Macphail, the engineer, and Sunny Jim remarked that a quite good gabbart lacking any obvious owners wasn't to be picked up every day. If they towed her up to Tighnabruaich they would have a very pretty claim for salvage.

"Fifty pounds at least for ship and cargo," said Macphail; "my share 'll pay for my flittin' at the term, jist nate."

"Fifty pounds!" said Para Handy. "It's a tidy sum, and there might be more than fifty in't when it came to the bit, for fifty pounds iss not an aawful lot when the owner gets his wheck of it. What do you think yoursel', Dougie?"

"I wass chust thinkin'," said Dougie, "that fifty pounds would be a terrible lot for poor MacCallum, him that owns the Katherine-Anne; he hasna been very lucky wi' her."

"If we're no' gaun to get the fifty pound then, we can just tow her up to Tighnabruaich for a baur," said Sunny Jim. "It doesna dae to be stickin'. If there's naething else in't, we'll get a' oor names in the papers for a darin' deed at sea. Come on, chaps, be game!"

"I wish to peace the Katherine-Anne belonged to any other man than John MacCallum," said the skipper. "You're an aawful cluver laad, Macphail; what iss the law aboot salvage?"

"Under the Merchant Shippin' Act," said Macphail glibly, "ye're bound to get your salvage; if ye divna claim't, it goes to the King the same as whales or onything that's cast up by the sea."

"Ach! it disna maitter a docken aboot the salvage," said Sunny Jim. "Look at the fun we'll hae comin' into Tighnabruaich wi' a boat we fun' the same as it was a kitlin. See's a rope, and I'll go on board and mak' her fast."

When they had towed the Katherine-Anne to Tighnabruaich, Dougie was sent ashore with a telegram for the owner of the *Vital Spark*, suggesting his immediate appearance on the scene. Later in the afternoon the crew of the Katherine-Anne came by steamer to Tighnabruaich, to which port she and they belonged, and the captain and owner ruefully surveyed the vessel he had abandoned, now lying safe and sound at his native quay. He sat on a barrel of paraffin-oil and looked at Para Handy in possession.

"Where did you pick her up?" said MacCallum sadly.

"Oh, chust doon the road a bit," said Para Handy. "It's clearin' up a nice day."

"It's a terrible business this," said MacCallum, nervously wiping his forehead with his handkerchief.

"Bless me! what is't?" exclaimed Para Handy. "I havena seen the paper this week yet."

"I mean about havin' to leave the Katie-Anne almost at our own door, and you finding her."

"Chust that; it wass Providence," remarked Para Handy piously, "chust Providence."

"I'll hae to gie you something for your bother," said MacCallum.

"I wouldna say but you would," replied the skipper. "It's a mercy your lifes wass saved. Hoo are they keepin', aal, in Ro'sa'?"

"Are ye no' comin' ashore for a dram?" remarked MacCallum, and Para cocked at him a cunning eye.

"No, John," he said; "I'm no' carin' mich aboot a dram the day;
I had wan yesterday."

But he succumbed to the genial impulse an hour later, and
leaving his mate in possession of the Katherine-Anne, went up the
village with the owner of that unhappy craft. MacCallum took
him to his home, where Para Handy found himself in the uncom-
fortable presence of a wife and three daughters dressmaking. The
four women sewed so assiduously, and were so moist about the
eyes with weeping, that he was sorry he came.

"This is the gentleman that found the Katie-Anne," remarked
MacCallum by way of introduction, and the eldest daughter
sobbed.

"Ye're aal busy!" said Para Handy, with a desperate air of cheer-
fulness.

"Indeed, aye! we're busy enough," said the mother bitterly.
"We're workin' oor fingers to the bane, but we're no' makin' much
o't; it's come wi' the wind and gang wi' the water," and the second
daughter sobbed in unison with her sister as they furiously plied
their needles.

"By Chove!" thought Para Handy, "a man would need to have
the he'rt o' a hoose-factor on a chob like this; it puts me aal oot
o' trum," and he drank his glass uncomfortably.

"I think ye mentioned aboot fifty pounds?" said MacCallum
mournfully, and at these words all the four women laid their
sewing on their knees and wept without restraint. "Fi-fi-fifty p-p-
pounds!" exclaimed the mother, "where in the wide world is John
MacCallum to get fifty pounds?"

Para Handy came hurriedly down the quay and called Dougie
ashore from the Katherine-Anne.

"Somebody must stay on board of her, or we'll have trouble wi'
the salvage," said the mate.

"Come ashore this meenute," commanded the Captain, "for
I'm needin' some refreshment. There's four women yonder greetin'
their eyes oot at the loss o' fifty pounds."

"Chust that!" said Dougie sympathetically. "Poor things!"

"I would see the salvage to the duvvle," said the Captain warmly,
"if we hadna sent that telegram to oor owner. Four o' them
sew-sew-sewing yonder and dreepin', like the fountain oot in Kelv-
ingrove!"

"Man, it wass lucky, too, aboot the telegram," said Dougie, "for
I didna like to send it and it's no' away."

Para Handy slapped him on the shoulder. "Man!" he said, "that's capital! To the muschief with their fifty pounds! Believe you me, I'm feelin' quite sublime!"

Chapter VII

PARA HANDY HAS AN EYE TO BUSINESS

It was a lovely day, and the *Vital Spark*, without a cargo, lay at the pier of Ormidale, her newly painted under-strakes reflected in a loch like a mirror, making a crimson blotch in a scene that was otherwise winter-brown. For a day and a half more there was nothing to be done. "It's the life of a Perfect Chentleman," said Dougie. The engineer, with a novelette he had bought in Glasgow, was lost in the love affairs of a girl called Gladys, who was excessively poor, but looked, at Chapter Five, like marrying a Colonel of Hussars who seemed to have no suspicion of the fate in store for him; and Sunny Jim, with the back of his head showing at the fo'c'sle scuttle, was making with his melodeon what sounded like a dastardly attack on "The Merry Widow."

"I wass thinkin', seein' we're here and nothing else doin', we might be givin' her the least wee bit touch o' the tar-brush," remarked Para Handy, who never cared to lose a chance of beautifying his vessel.

"There it is again!" exclaimed Macphail, laying down his novelette in exasperation. "A chap canna get sittin' doon five meenutes in this boat for a read to himsel' withoot somebody breakin' their legs to find him a job. Ye micht as weel be in a man-o'-war." Even Dougie looked reproachfully at the Captain; he had just been about to pull his cap down over his eyes and have a little sleep before his tea.

"It wass only a proposeetion," said the Captain soothingly. "No offence! Maybe it'll do fine when we get to Tarbert. It's an awfu' peety they're no' buildin' boats o' this size wi' a kind of a study in them for the use o' the enchineers," and he turned for sympathy to the mate, who was usually in the mood to rag Macphail. But this time Dougie was on Macphail's side.

"There's some o' your jokes like the Carradale funerals — there's no' much fun in them," he remarked. "Ye think it's great sport to be tar-tar-tarring away at the ship; ye never consult either oor healths or oor inclinations. Am I right, Macphail?"

"Slave-drivin'! that's whit I ca't," said Macphail emphatically. "If Lloyd George kent aboot it, he would bring it before the Board o' Tred."

The Captain withdrew, moodily, from his crew, and ostentatiously scraped old varnish off the mast. This business engaged him only for a little; the weather was so plainly made for idleness that he speedily put the scraper aside and entered into discourse with Sunny Jim. "Whatever you do, don't you be a Captain, Jum," he advised him.

"I wisht I got the chance!" said Sunny Jim.

"There's nothing in't but the honor o' the thing, and a shilling or two extra; no' enough to pay the drinks to keep up the poseetion. Here am I, and I'm anxious to be frien'ly wi' the chaps, trate them the same's I wass their equal, and aalways ready to come-and-go a bit, and they go and give me the name o' a slave-driver! Iss it no' chust desperate?"

"If I was a Captain," said Sunny Jim philosophically, "I wad dae the comin' and mak' the ither chaps dae the goin', and d — d smert aboot it."

"That's aal right for a Gleska man, but it's no' the way we're brocht up on Loch Long; us Arrochar folk, when we're Captains, believe in a bit o' compromise wi' the crews. If they don't do a thing when we ask them cuvilly, we do't oorsel's, and that's the way to vex them."

"Did ye never think ye wad like to change your job and try something ashore?" asked Sunny Jim.

"Many a time!" confessed the Captain. "There's yonder jobs that would suit me fine. I wass nearly, once, an innkeeper. It wass at a place called Cladich; the man came into a puckle money wi' his wife, and advertised the goodwull at a great reduction. I left the boat for a day and walked across to see him. He wass a man they caalled MacDiarmid, and he wass yonder wi' his sleeves up puttin' corks in bottles wi' a wonderful machine. Did you ever see them corkin' bottles, Jum?"

"I never noticed if I did," said Sunny Jim; "but I've seen them takin' them oot."

"Chust that! This innkeeper wass corkin' away like hey-my-nanny.

"'You're sellin' the business?' says I.

"'I am,' says he; and him throng corkin' away at the bottles.

"'What's your price?' says I.

"'A hundred and fifty pounds for the goodwull and the stock the way it stands,' says he.

"'What aboot the fixtures?' then says I.

"'Oh, they're aal right!" said the innkeeper, cork-cork-corkin' away at the bottles; 'the fixtures goes along with the goodwull.'

"'What fixtures iss there?' says I.

"'There's three sheep termers, the shoemaker doon the road, and Macintyre the mail-driver, and that's no' coontin' a lot o' my Sunday customers,' said the innkeeper."

"You didna tak' the business, then?" said Sunny Jim.

"Not me!" said Para Handy. "To be corkin' away at bottles aal my lone yonder would put me crazy. Forbye, I hadna the half o' the hunder-and-fifty. There wass another time I went kind o' into a business buyin' eggs —"

"Eggs!" exclaimed Sunny Jim with some astonishment — "whit kin' o' eggs?"

"Och! chust egg eggs," said the Captain. "It wass a man in Arran said there wass a heap o' money in them if you had the talent and a wee bit powney to go roond the countryside. To let you ken: it wass before the *Fital Spark* changed owners; the chentleman that had her then wass a wee bit foolish; nothing at aal against his moral and releegious reputaation, mind, but apt to go over the score with it, and forget whereaboots the vessel would be lying. This time we were for a week or more doin' nothin' in Loch Ranza, and waitin' for his orders. He couldna mind for the life o' him where he sent us, and wass telegraphin' aal the harbor-masters aboot the coast to see if they kent the whereaboots o' the *Fital Spark*, but it never came into his heid that we might be near Loch Ranza, and there we were wi' the best o' times doin' nothing."

"Could ye no' hae sent him a telegraph tellin' him where ye wiz?" asked Sunny Jim.

"That's what he said himsel', but we're no' that daft, us folk from Arrochar; I can tell you we have aal oor faculties. Dougie did better than that; he put a bit o' paper in a bottle efter writin' on't a message from the sea — 'S.S. *Fital Spark* stranded for a fortnight in a fit o' absent-mind; aal hands quite joco, but the owner lost.'

"We might have been lyin' in Loch Ranza yet if it wassna that I tried Peter Carmichael's business. 'When you're doin' nothing better here,' he said to me, 'you micht be makin' your fortune buyin' and sellin' eggs, for Arran's fair hotchin' wi' them.'

"'What way do you do it?' says I.

"'You need a wee cairt and a powney,' said Peter Carmichael, 'and I've the very cairt and powney that would suit you. You go roond the island gatherin' eggs from aal the hooses, and pay them sixpence a dozen — champion eggs ass fresh ass the mornin' breeze. Then you pack them in boxes and send them to Gleska and sell them at a profit.'

"'What profit do you chenerally allow yoursel'?' I asked Peter.

"'Oh! chust nate wan percent,' said Peter; 'you chairge a shillin' in Gleska for the eggs; rale Arran eggs, no' foreign rubbadge. Folk 'll tell you to put your money in stone and lime; believe me, nothing bates the Arran egg for quick returns. If the people in Gleska have a guarantee that any parteecular egg wass made in Arran, they'll pay any money for it; it's ass good ass a day at the coast for them, poor craturs!'

"Seein' there wass no prospeck o' the owner findin' where we were unless he sent a bloodhound oot to look for us, I asked Carmichael hoo long it would take to learn the business, and he said I could pick it up in a week. I agreed to buy the cairt and powney and the goodwull o' the business if the chob at the end o' the week wass like to bring in a pleasin' wage, and Dougie himsel' looked efter the shup. You never went roond the country buyin' eggs? It's a chob you need a lot o' skill for. Yonder wass Peter Carmichael and me goin' roond by Pirnmill, Machrie, and Black-waterfoot, Sliddery, and Shiskine —"

"Ach! ye're coddin'!" exclaimed Sunny Jim; "there's no such places."

"It's easy seen you were a' your days on the Clutha steamers," said the Captain patiently; "I'll assure you that there's Sli:derys and Shiskines oot in Arran. Full o' eggs! The hens oot yonder's no' puttin' bye their time!

"Three days runnin' Peter and me and the powney scoured the country and gaithered so many eggs that I begun to get rud in the face whenever I passed the least wee hen. We couldna get boxes enough to hold them in Loch Ranza, so we got some bales o' hay and packed them in the hold of the *Fital Spark*, and then con-sudered. 'There's nothing to do noo but to take them to the Broomielaw and sell them quick at a shillin',' said Carmichael. 'The great thing iss to keep them on the move, and off your hands before they change their minds and start for to be chuekens. Up steam, smert, and off wi' ye! And here's the cairt and powney — fifteen pounds.'

"'Not at aal, Carmichael!' I said to him; 'I'll wait till I'll see if you wass right aboot the wan percent of profits. Stop you here till I'll come back.'

"I telegraphed that day to the owner o' the vessel, sayin' I was comin' into the Clyde wi' a cargo, and when we got to Gleska he wass standin' on the quay, and not in the best o' trum.

"'Where in a' the world were you?' says he; 'and me lookin' high and low for you! What's your cargo?'

"'Eggs from Arran, Mr. Smuth,' says I, 'and a bonny job I had gettin' them at sixpence the dozen.'

"'Who are they from?' he asked, glowerin' under the hatches.

"'Chust the cheneral population, Mr. Smuth,' says I.

"'Who are they consigned to?' he asked then — and man he wassna in trum at aal, at aal!

"'Anybody that'll buy them, sir," said I; 'it's a bit of a speculation.'

"He scratched his heid and looked at me. 'I mind o' orderin' eggs,' says he, 'but I never dreamt I wass daft enough to send for a boat-load o' them. But noo they're here I suppose we'll have to make the best o' them.' So he sold the eggs, and kept the wan percent for freight and responsibeelity, and I made nothin' off it except that I shifted my mind aboot takin' a chob ashore, and didn't buy Carmichael's cairt and powney."

A VEGETARIAN EXPERIMENT

*T*he *Vital Spark* had been lying for some time in the Clyde getting in a new boiler, and her crew, who had been dispersed about the city in their respective homes, returned to the wharf on a Monday morning to make ready for a trip to Tobermory.

"She's a better boat than ever she was," said Macphail with satisfaction, having made a casual survey. "Built like a lever watch! We'll can get the speed oot o' her noo. There's boats gaun up and doon the river wi' red funnels, saloon caibins, and German bands in them, that havena finer engines. When I get that crank and crossheid tightened, thae glands packed and nuts slacked, she'll be the gem o' the sea."

"She's chust sublime!" said Para Handy, patting the tarred old hull as if he were caressing a kitten; "it's no' coals and timber she should be carryin' at aal, but towrist passengers. Man! if we chust had the accommodation!"

"Ye should hae seen the engines we had on the Cluthas!" remarked Sunny Jim, who had no illusions about the *Vital Spark* in that respect. "They were that shiney I could see my face in them."

"Could ye, 'faith?" said Macphail; "a sicht like that must have put ye aff yer work. We're no' that fond o' polish in the coastin' tred that we mak' oor engines shine like an Eyetalian ice-cream shop; it's only vanity. Wi' us it's speed —"

"Eight knots," murmured Sunny Jim, who was in a nasty Monday-moming humor. "Eight knots, and the chance o' nine wi' wind and tide."

"You're a liar!" said the Captain irritably, "and that's my advice to you. Ten knots many a time between the Cloch and the Holy Isle," and an argument ensued which it took Dougie all his tact to put an end to short of bloodshed.

"It's me that's gled to be back on board of her anyway," remarked Para Handy later; "I suppose you'll soon be gettin' the dinner ready, Jum? See and have something nice, for I'm tired o' sago puddin'."

"Capital stuff for pastin' up bills," said Dougie; "I've seen it often in the cookin'-depots. Wass the wife plyin' ye wi' sago?"

"Sago, and apples, potatoes, cabbage, cheese, and a new kind o' patent coffee that agrees wi' the indigestion; I havena put my two eyes on a bit of Christian beef since I went ashore; the wife's in wan of her tirravees, and she's turned to be a vegetarian."

"My Chove!" said Dougie incredulously; "are you sure, Peter?"

"Sure enough! I told her this mornin' when I left I would bring her home a bale of hay from Mull, and it would keep her goin' for a month or two. Women's a curious article!"

"You should get the munister to speak to her," said Dougie sympathetically. "When a wife goes wrong like that, there's nothing bates the munister. She'll no' be goin' to the church; it's aalways the way wi' them fancy new releegions. Put you her at wance in the hands o' a dacent munister."

"I canna be harsh wi' her, or she'll greet," said Para Handy sadly.

"It's no harshness that's wanted," counseled the mate, speaking from years of personal experience; "what you need iss to be firm. What way did this calamity come on her? Don't be standin' there,

Jum, like a soda-water bottle, but hurry and make a bit of steak for the Captain; man! I noticed you werena in trum whenever I saw you come on board. I saw at wance you hadn't the agility. What way did the trouble come on her?"

"She took it off a neighbor woman," explained the Captain. "She wass aal right on the Sunday, and on the Monday mornin' she couldna bear to look at ham and eggs. It might happen to anybody. The thing was at its heid when I got home, and the only thing on the table wass a plate of maccaroni."

"Eyetalian!" chimed in the engineer. "I've seen them makin' it in Genoa and hingin' it up to bleach on the washin'-greens. It's no' meat for men; it's only for passin' the time o' organ-grinders and ship-riggers."

"'Mery,' I said to her, 'I never saw nicer decorations, but hurry up like a darlin' wi' the meat.' 'There'll be no more meat in this hoose, Peter,' she said, aal trumblin'; 'if you saw them busy in a slaughter-hoose you wadna eat a chop. Forbye, there's uric acid in butcher meat, and there's more nourishment in half a pound o' beans than there iss in half a bullock.' 'That's three beans for a sailor's dinner; it's no' for nourishment a man eats always; half the time it's only for amusement, Mery,' said I to her, but it wass not the time for argyment. 'You'll be a better man in every way if you're a vegetarian,' she said to me. 'If it iss a better man you are wantin',' I says to her, wonderful caalm in my temper, 'you are on the right tack, sure enough; you have only to go on with them expuriments wi' my meat and you'll soon be a weedow woman.'

"But she wouldna listen to reason, Mery, and for a fortnight back I have been feedin' like the Scribes and Sadducees in the Scruptures."

"Man! iss it no chust desperate?" said Dougie compassionately, and he admiringly watched his Captain a little later make the first hearty meal for a fortnight. "You're lookin' a dufferent man already," he told him; "what's for the tea, Jum?"

"I kent a vegetarian yince," said Sunny Jim, "and he lived maist o' the time on chuckle soup."

"Chucken soup?" repeated Dougie interrogatively.

"No; chuckie soup. There was nae meat o' ony kind in't. A' ye needed was some vegetables, a pot o' hot water, and a parteecular kind o' chuckie-stane. It was fine and strengthenin'."

"You would need good teeth for't, I'm thinkin'," remarked the Captain dubiously.

"Of course ye didna eat the chuckie-stane," Sunny Jim explained; "it made the stock; it was instead o' a bane, and it did ower and ower again."

"It would be a great savin'," said Dougie, fascinated with the idea. "Where do you get them parteecular kinds ofchuckies?"

"Onywhere under high water," replied Sunny Jim, who saw prospects of a little innocent entertainment.

"We'll get them the first time we're ashore, then," said the mate, "and if they're ass good ass what you say, the Captain could take home a lot of them for his vegetarian mustress."

At the first opportunity, when he got ashore. Sunny Jim perambulated the beach and selected a couple of substantial pieces of quartz, and elsewhere bought a pound of margarine which he put in his pocket. "Here yez are, chaps — the very chuckie! I'll soon show ye soup," he said, coming aboard with the stones, in which the crew showed no little interest. "A' ye have to do is to scrub them weel, and put them in wi' the vegetables when the pot's boilin'."

They watched his culinary preparations closely. He prepared the water and vegetables, cleaned the stones, and solemnly popped them in the pot when the water boiled. At a moment when their eyes were off him he dexterously added the unsuspected pound of margarine. By and by the soup was ready, and when dished, had all the aspect of the ordinary article. Sunny Jim himself was the first to taste it pour encourager les autres. "Fair champion!" he exclaimed. The engineer could not be prevailed to try the soup on any consideration, but the Captain and the mate had a plate apiece, and voted it extraordinary.

"It's a genius you are, Jum!" said the delighted Captain; "if the folk in Gleska knew that soup like this was to be made from chuckie-stanes they wouldna waste their time at the Fair wi' gaitherin' cockles."

And the next time Para Handy reached the Clyde he had on board in all good faith a basket-load of stones culled from the beach at Tobermory for his vegetarian mistress.

THE COMPLETE GENTLEMAN

"*T*he finest chentleman I ever knew was Hurricane Jeck," said Para Handy. "His manners wass complete. Dougie himsel' will tell you."

"A nice laad," said the mate agreeably; "he had a great, great faculty."

— "Whaur did he mak' his money?" asked Sunny Jim, and they looked at him with compassion.

"There iss men that iss chentlemen, and there iss men that hass a puckle money," said the Captain impressively; "Hurricane Jeck wass seldom very rife with money, but he came from Kinlochaline, and that iss ass good ass a Board of Tred certuficate. Stop you till you're long enough on the *Fital Spark*, and you'll get your educaation. Hurricane Jeck was a chentleman. What money he had he would spend like the wave of the sea."

"It didna maitter wha's money it was, either," chimed in Macphail unsympathetically. "I kent him! Fine!"

"Like the wave of the sea," repeated the Captain, meeting the engineer's qualification with the silence of contempt. "Men like Jeck should never be oot of money, they distribute it with such a taste."

"I've seen chaps like that," remarked Sunny Jim, who was sympathetic to that kind of character. "When I was on the Cluthas —"

"When you was on the Cluthas, Jum, you were handlin' nothing but ha'pennies; Hurricane Jeck wass a chentleman in pound notes, and that's the dufference."

"My Jove!" said Sunny Jim, "he must hae been weel an'!"

"There wass wan time yonder," proceeded the Captain, "when Jeck came into a lot o' money from a relative that died — fifty pounds if it wass a penny, and he spent it in a manner that was chust sublime. The very day he got it, he came down to the *Fital Spark* at Bowlin' for a consultation. 'You'll no' guess what's the trouble, Peter,' said he; 'I'm a chentleman of fortune,' and he spread the fifty notes fornent him, with a bit of stone on each of them to keep them doon, the same as it wass a bleachin'-green. 'Fifty pounds and a fortnight to spend it in, before we sail for

China. Put bye your boat, put on your Sunday clothes, and you and me'll have a little recreaation.'

"'I canna, Jeck,' says I — and Dougie himsel' 'll tell you — 'I canna, Jeck; the cargo's in, and we're sailin' in the mornin'.'

"'That's the worst o' money," said Hurricane Jeck; 'there's never enough o't. If Uncle Willy had left me plenty I would buy your boat and no' let a cargo o' coals interfere wi' oor diversion.'

"'Put it in the bank,' I said to him.

"'I'm no' that daft,' he said. 'There's no' a worst place in the world for money than the banks; you never get the good o't."

"'Oh, there's plenty of other ways of gettin' rid of it,' I told him.

"'Not of fifty pounds,' said Jeck. 'It's easy spendin' a pound or two, but you canna get rid o' a legacy withoot assistance.' Wassn't that the very words of him, Dougie?"

"Chust his own words!" said the mate; "your memory iss capital."

"'There's a lot o' fun I used to think I would indulge in if I had the money,' said Hurricane Jeck, 'and now I have the opportunity if I only had a friend like yoursel' to see me doin' it. I'm goin' to spend it aal in trevellin'.'"

"And him a sailor!" commented the astonished Sunny Jim.

"He wass meanin' trevellin' on shore," said Para Handy. "Trains, and tramway cars, and things like that, and he had a brulliant notion. It wass aye a glief to Jeck that there wass so many things ashore you darena do withoot a prosecution. 'The land o' the Free!' he would say,' and ye canna take a tack on a train the length o' Paisley withoot a bit of a pasteboard ticket!' He put in the rest of that day that I speak of trevellin' the Underground till he wass dizzy, and every other hour he had an altercaation wi' the railway folk aboot his ticket. 'Take it oot o' that,' he would tell them, handin' them a pound or two, and he quite upset the traffic. On the next day he got a Gladstone bag, filled it with empty bottles, and took the train to Greenock. 'Don't throw bottles oot at the windows,' it says in the railway cairrages; Jeck opened the windows and slipped oot a bottle or two at every quarter mile, till the Caledonian system looked like the mornin' efter a Good Templars' trip. They catched him doin' it at Pollokshields.

"'What's the damage?' he asked them, hangin' his arm on the inside strap o' a first-cless cairrage and smokin' a fine cigar. You never saw a fellow that could be more genteel.

"'It might be a pound a bottle,' said the railway people; 'we have the law for it.'

"'Any reduction on takin' a quantity?' said Jeck; 'I'm havin' the time o' my life; it's most refreshin'.'

"That day he took the train to Edinburgh – didn't he, Dougie?"

"He did that!" said Dougie. "You have the story exactly."

"He took the train to Edinburgh. It was an express, and every noo and then he would pull the chain communication wi' the guard. The train would stop, and the guard would come and talk with Jeck. The first time he came along Jeck shook him by the hand, and said he only wanted to congratulate him.

"'What aboot?' said the guard, no' lookin' very well pleased.

"'On your cheneral agility,' said Hurricane Jeck. 'Your cairrages iss first-rate; your speed iss astonishin' quick; your telegraph communication iss workin' A1; and you stopped her in two lengths. I thocht I would chust like you to take my compliments to the owners.'

"'It's five pounds o' a fine for pullin' the cord,' said the guard.

"'That's only for the wan cord; I pulled the two o' them,' said Jeck, quite nice to him; 'first the port and then the starboard. You canna be too parteecular. There's the money and a shillin' extra for a dram.'

"The guard refused the money, and said he would see aboot it at Edinburgh, and the train went on. Jeck pulled the cords till he had them all in the cairrage wi' him, but the train never stopped till it came to Edinburgh, and then a score o' the offeecials came to the cairrage.

"'What are you doin' with them cords?' they asked him.

"'Here they are, all coiled up and flemished-down,' said Jeck, lightin' another cigar. 'When does this train go back?' and he hands them over a bunch o' notes, and told them never to mind the change."

"Man! he was the comic!" exclaimed Sunny Jim. "Fair champion!"

"In Edinburgh," proceeded Pary Handy, "he waalked aboot till he came on a fire alarm where it said it would cost a heavy fine to work it unless there wass a fire. Jeck rung the bell, and waited whustlin' till the Fire Brigade came clatterin' up the street.

"'Two meenutes and fifty seconds,' he says to them, holdin' his watch; 'they couldna do better in Gleska. I like your helmets. Noo that we're aal here, what iss it goin' to be, boys?'

"'Are you drunk, or daft?' said the Captain o' the Fire Brigade, grippin' him by the collar.

"'Not a drop since yesterday!' said Jeck. 'And I'm no' daft, but chust an honest Brutish sailor, puttin' bye the time and spreadin' aboot my money. There's me and there's Mr. Carnegie. His hobby is libraries; on the other hand I'm for Liberty. The Land of the Free and the Brave; it says on the fire alarm that I mustna break it, and I proved I could. Take your money oot o' that,' — and he hands the Captain the bundle of notes. 'If there iss any change left when you pay yoursel's for your bother, send home the enchines and we'll aal adjourn to a place.'"

"Capital!" exclaimed Dougie.

"It took three days for Jeck to get rid of his fortune in cheneral amusement of that kind, and then he came to see me before he joined his shup for China.

"'I had a fine time, Peter,' he said; 'couldna have better. You would wonder the way the week slipped by. But it's the Land of the Free, right enough; there's no' half enough o' laws a chentleman can break for his diversion; I hadna very mich of a selection.'"

AN OCEAN TRAGEDY

*I*t was a lovely afternoon at the end of May, and the *Vital Spark* was puffing down Kilbrannan Sound with a farmer's flitting. Macphail, the engineer, sat "with his feet among the enchines and his heid in the clouds," as Dougie put it — in other words, on the ladder of his engine-room, with his perspiring brow catching the cool breeze made by the vessel's progress, and his emotions rioting through the adventures of a governess in the 'Family Herald Supplement.' Peace breathed like an exhalation from the starboard hills; the sea was like a mirror, broken only by the wheel of a stray porpoise, and Sunny Jim indulged the Captain and the mate with a medley on his melodeon.

"You're a capital player, Jum," said the Captain in a pause of the entertainment. "Oh, yes, there's no doot you are cluver on it; it's a gift, but you havena the selection; no, you havena the selection, and if you havena the selection where are you?"

"He's doin' his best," said Dougie sympathetically, and then, in one of those flashes of philosophy that come to the most thoughtless of us at times — "A man can do no more."

"Whit selections was ye wantin'?" asked the musician, with a little irritation; "if it's Gaelic sangs ye're meanin' I wad need a drum and the nicht aff."

"No, I wassna thinkin' aboot Gaalic sangs," explained Para Handy; "when we're consuderin' them we're consuderin' music; I wass taalkin' of the bits of things you put on the melodeon; did you ever hear 'Napoleon'?" and clearing his throat he warbled —

"Wa-a-an night sad and dree-ary Ass I lay on my bed, And my head scarce reclined on the pillow; A vision surprisin' came into my head, And I dreamt I wass crossin' the billow. And ass my proud vessel she dashed o'er the deep —"

"It wasna the *Vital Spark*, onywye," remarked Macphail cynically; "afore I got her biler sorted she couldna dash doon a waterfall —"

"I beheld a rude rock, it was craggy and steep,"
(proceeded the vocalist, paying no attention),
"'Twas the rock where the willow iss now seen to weep, O'er the grave of the once-famed Napo-o-o-ole-on!"

"I never heard better, Peter," said the mate approvingly. "Take your breath and give us another touch of it. There's nothing bates the old songs."

"Let me see, noo, what wass the second verse?" asked the Captain, with his vanity as an artist fully roused; "it was something like this —

"And ass my proud vessel she near-ed the land, I beheld clad in green, his bold figure; The trumpet of fame clasped firm in his hand, On his brow there wass valor and vigor."

"Balloons! balloons!" cried Macphail, mutating some Glasgow street barrow-vendor. "Fine balloons for rags and banes."

"Fair do! gie the Captain a chance," expostulated Sunny Jim. "Ye're daein' fine. Captain; Macphail's jist chawed because he canna get readin'."

"'Oh, stranger,' he cried,' dost thou come unto me, From the land of thy fathers who boast they are free; Then, if so, a true story I'll tell unto thee Concerning myself — I'm Napo-o-o-ole-on,'"

proceeded the Captain, no way discouraged, and he had no sooner concluded the final doleful note than a raucous voice from the uncovered hold cried "Co-co-coals!"

Even Dougie sniggered; Macphail fell into convulsions of laughter, and Sunny Jim showed symptoms of choking.

"I can stand Macphail's umpudence, but I'll no' stand that nonsense from a hoolit on my own shup," exclaimed the outraged vocalist, and, stretching over the coamings, he grabbed from the top of a chest of drawers in the hold a cage with a cockatoo. "Come oot like a man," said he, "and say't again."

"Toots! Peter, it's only a stupid animal; I wouldna put myself a bit aboot," remarked Dougie soothingly. "It's weel enough known them cockatoos have no ear for music. Forbye, he wassna meanin' anything when he cried 'Coals!' he was chust in fun."

"Fun or no," said Macphail, "a bird wi' sense like that's no' canny. Try him wi' another verse. Captain, and see if he cries on the polls."

"If he says another word I'll throw him over the side," said Para Handy. "It's nothing else but mutiny," and with a wary eye on the unsuspecting cockatoo he sang another verse —

"'You remember that year so immortal,' he cried, 'When I crossed the rude Alps famed in story, With the legions of France, for her sons were my pride, And I led them to honor and glory —'"

"Oh, crickey! Chase me, girls!" exclaimed the cockatoo, and the next moment was swinging over the side of the *Vital Spark* to a watery grave.

The fury of the outraged Captain lasted but a moment; he had the vessel stopped and the punt out instantly for a rescue; but the unhappy bird was irrecoverably gone, and the tea-hour on the *Vital Spark* that afternoon was very melancholy. Macphail, particularly, was inexpressibly galling in the way he over and over again brought up the painful topic.

"I canna get it oot o' my heid," he said; "the look it gied when ye were gaun to swing it roon' your heid and gie't the heave! I'll cairry that cockatoo's last look to my grave."

"Whit kin' o' look was it?" asked Sunny Jim, eager for details; "I missed it."

"It was a look that showed ye the puir bird kent his last oor was come," explained the engineer. "It wasna anger, and it wasna exactly fricht; it was — man! I canna picture it to ye, but efter this ye needna tell me beasts have nae sowls; it's a' my aunty. Yon bird —"

"I wish I hadna put a finger on him," said the Captain, sore stricken with remorse. "Change the subject."

"The puir bird didna mean ony hairm," remarked Sunny Jim, winking at the engineer. "'Coals!' or 'Chase me, girls!' is jist a thing onybody would say if they heard a chap singin' a sang like yon; it's oot o' date. Fair do! ye shouldna hae murdered the beast; the man it belangs to 'll no' be awfu' weel pleased."

"Murdered the beast!" repeated the conscience-stricken Captain; "it's no' a human body you're talkin' aboot," and the engineer snorted his amazement.

"Michty! Captain, is that a' ye ken?" he exclaimed. "If it's no' murder, it's manslaughter; monkeys, cockatoos, and parrots a' come under the Act o' Parliament. A cockatoo's no' like a canary; it's able to speak the language and give an opeenion, and the man that wad kill a cockatoo wad kill a wean."

"That's right enough, Peter," said Dougie pathetically; "everybody kens it's manslaughter. I never saw a nicer cockatoo either; no' a better behaved bird; it's an awful peety. Perhaps the polis at Carradale will let the affair blow bye."

"I wassna meanin' to henn the bird," pleaded Para Handy. "It aggravated me. Here wass I standin' here singin' 'Napoleon,' and the cockatoo wass yonder, and he hurt my feelin's twice; you would be angry yoursel' if it wass you. My nerves got the better o' me."

"If the polls cross-examine me," said the engineer emphatically, "I'll conceal naething, I'll no' turn King's evidence or onything like that, mind, but if I'm asked I'll tell the truth, for I don't want to be mixed up wi' a case o' manslaughter and risk my neck."

Thus were the feelings of the penitent Para Handy lacerated afresh every hour of the day, till he would have given everything he possessed in the world to restore the cockatoo to life. The owner's anger at the destruction of his bird was a trifle to be anticipated calmly; the thought that made Para Handy's heart like lead was that cockatoos *did* speak, that this one even seemed to have the gift of irony, and that he had drowned a fellow-being; it was, in fact, he admitted to himself, a kind of manslaughter. His shipmates found a hundred ways of presenting his terrible deed to him in fresh aspects.

"Cockatoos iss mentioned in the Scruptures," said Dougie; "I don't exactly mind the place, but I've seen it."

"They live mair nor a hundred years if they're weel trated," was Sunny Jim's contribution to the natural history of the bird.

"Naebody ever saw a deid cockatoo," added the engineer.

"I wish you would talk aboot something else," said the Captain piteously; "I'm troubled enough in mind withoot you bringin' that accursed bird up over and over again," and they apologized, but always came back to the topic again.

"I wid plead guilty and throw mysel' on the mercy o' the coort," was Macphail's suggestion. "At the maist it'll no' be mair nor a sentence for life."

"Ye could say ye did it in self-defense," recommended Sunny Jim. "Thae cockatoos bites hke onything."

"A great calamity!" moaned Dougie, shaking his head.

When the cargo of furniture was discharged and delivered, the farmer discovered the absence of his cockatoo, and came down to make inquiries.

"He fell over the side," was the Captain's explanation. "We had his cage hanging on the shrouds, and a gale struck us and blew it off. His last words wass, 'There's nobody to blame but mysel'.'"

"There was no gale aboot here," said the farmer, suspecting nothing. "I'm gey sorry to lose that cage. It was a kind o' a pity, too, the cockatoo bein' drooned."

"Say nothing aboot that," pleaded the Captain. "I have been moumin' about that cockatoo all week; you wouldna believe the worry it haas been for me, and when all iss said and done I consider the cockatoo had the best of it."

THE RETURN OF THE TAR

A yachtsman with "R.Y.S. *Dolphin*" blazoned on his guernsey came down Campbeltown quay and sentimentally regarded the *Vital Spark*, which had just completed the discharge of a cargo of coals under circumstances pleasing to her crew, since there had been a scarcity of carts, two days of idleness, and two days' demurrage. Para Handy saw him looking — "The smartest shup in the tred," he remarked to Sunny Jim; "you see the way she catches their eye! It's her lines, and cheneral appearance; stop you till I give her a touch of paint next month!"

"He'll ken us again when he sees us," said Sunny Jim, unpleasantly conscious of his own grimy aspect, due to eight hours of coal dust. "Hey, you wi' the sign-board, is't a job you're wantin'?" he cried to the yachtsman; and started to souse himself in a bucket of water.

The stranger pensively gazed at the Captain, and said, "Does your eyes deceive me or am I no' Colin?"

"Beg pardon!" replied the Captain cautiously.

"Colin," repeated the stranger. "Surely you must mind The Tar?"

"Holy smoke!" exclaimed Para Handy, "you're no' my old shupmate, surely; if you are, there's a desperate change on you. Pass me up my spy-gless, Dougie."

The yachtsman jumped on board, and barely escaped crashing into the tea-dishes with which Sunny Jim proposed to deal when his toilet was completed. "And there's Dougie himsel'," he genially remarked; "– and Macphail, too; it's chust like comin' home. Are ye aal in good condeetion?"

"We canna complain," said Dougie, shaking the proffered hand with some dubiety. "If you were The Tar we used to have you wouldna miss them plates so handy wi' your feet." They stood around and eyed him shrewdly; he certainly looked a little like The Tar if The Tar could be imagined wideawake, trim, cleanshaven, and devoid of diffidence. The engineer, with a fancy nourished on twenty years' study of novelettes, where fraudulent claimants to fortunes and estates were continually turning up, concluded at once that this was really not The Tar at all, but a clever impersonator, and wondered what the game was. The Captain took up a position more non-committal; he believed he could easily test the bona-fides of the stranger.

"And how's your brother Charles?" he inquired innocently.

"Cherles," said the yachtsman, puzzled. "I never had a brother Cherles."

"Neither you had, when I mind, now; my mistake!" said the Captain; "I wass thinkin' on another hand we used to have that joined the yats. Wass I not at your mairrage over in Colintraive?"

"I wasna mairried in Colintraive at all!" exclaimed the puzzled visitor. "Man, Captain! but your memory's failin'."

"Neither you were," agreed the Captain, thinking for a moment. "It wass such a cheery weddin', I forgot."

"If you're the oreeginal Tar," broke in the engineer, "you'll maybe gie me back my knife: ye mind I gied ye a len' o't the day ye left, and I didna get it back frae ye," but this was an accusation the visitor emphatically denied.

"You'll maybe no' hae an anchor tattooed aboot you anywhere?" asked the mate. "It runs in my mind there wass an anchor."

"Two of them," said the visitor, promptly baring an arm, and revealing these interesting decorations.

"That's anchors right enough," said the Captain, closely examining them, and almost convinced. "I canna say mysel' I mind o' them, but there they are, Dougie."

"It's easy tattooin' anchors," said the engineer; "whaur's your strawberry mark?"

"What's a strawberry mark?" asked the baffled stranger.

"There!" exclaimed Macphail triumphantly. "Everybody kens ye need to hae a strawberry mark. Hoo are we to ken ye're the man ye say ye are if ye canna produce a strawberry mark?" And again the confidence of the Captain was obviously shaken.

"Pass me along that pail," said the mate suddenly to the stranger, who, with his hands in his pockets, slid the pail along the deck to the petitioner with a lazy thrust of his foot that was unmistakably familiar.

The Captain slapped him on the shoulder. "It's you yoursel', Colin!" he exclaimed. "There wass never another man at sea had the same agility wi' his feet; it's me that's gled to see you. Many a day we missed you. It's chust them fancy togs that makes the difference. That and your hair cut, and your face washed so parteecular."

"A chentleman's life," said The Tar, later, sitting on a hatch with his bona-fides now established to the satisfaction of all but the engineer, who couldn't so readily forget the teachings of romance. "A chentleman's life. That's oor yat oot there; she comes from Cowes, and I'm doin' fine on her. I knew the tarry old hooker here ass soon ass I saw her at the quay."

"You're maybe doin' fine on the yats," said the Captain coldly, "but it doesna improve the mainners. She wassna a tarry old hooker when you were earnin' your pound a-week on her."

"No offence!" said The Tar remorsefully. "I wass only in fun. I've seen a wheen o' vessels since I left her, but none that had her style nor nicer shupmates."

"That's the truth!" agreed the Captain, mollified immediately. "Come doon and I'll show you the same old bunk you did a lot o' sleepin' in," and The Tar agreeably followed him with this sentimental purpose. They were below ten minutes, during which time the engineer summed up the whole evidence for and against the identity of the claimant, and proclaimed his belief to Dougie that the visitor had come to the *Vital Spark* after no good. He was so righteously indignant at what he considered a deception that he even refused to join the party when it adjourned into the town to celebrate the occasion fittingly at the Captain's invitation.

The Tar retired to his yacht in due course; Para Handy, Dougie, and Sunny Jim returned, on their part, to the *Vital Spark*, exhilarated to the value of half-a-crown handsomely disbursed by the Captain, who had never before been seen with a shilling of his own so far on in the week. They were met on board by Macphail in a singularly sarcastic frame of mind, mingled with a certain degree of restrained indignation.

"I hope your frien' trated ye well," he said.

"Fine!" said the Captain. "Colin was aye the chentleman. He's doin' capital on the yats."

"He'll be daein' time oot o' the yats afore he's done," said the engineer. "I kent he was efter nae guid comin' here, and when ye had him doon below showin' him whaur The Tar bunked, he picked my Sunday pocket o' hauf-a-croon. The man's a fraud, ye're blin' no' to see't; he hadna even a strawberry mark."

"Whatever you say yoursel'," replied the Captain, with an expansive wink at the mate and Sunny Jim. "If he's not The Tar, and took your money, it wass lucky you saw through him."

THE FORTUNE-TELLER

*T*arbert Fair was in full swing; the crew of the *Vital Spark* had exhausted the delirious delights of the hobby-horses, the shooting-gallery, Aunt Sally, Archer's Lilliputian Circus, and the booth where, after ten, they got pink fizzing drinks that had "a fine, fine appearance, but not mich fun in them," as Para Handy put it, and Dougie stumbled upon a gypsy's cart on the outskirts of the Fair, where a woman was telling fortunes. Looking around to assure himself that he was unobserved by the others, he went behind the cart tilt and consulted the oracle, a proceeding which took ten minutes, at the end of which time he rejoined the Captain, betraying a curious mood of alternate elation and depression.

"Them high-art fizzy drinks iss not agreeing with you, Dougie," said the Captain sympathetically; "you're losing all your joviality, and it not near the mornin'. Could you not get your eye on Macphail? I'll wudger he'll have something sensible in a bottle!"

"Macphail!" exclaimed the mate emphatically; "I wouldna go for a drink to him if I wass dyin'; I wouldna be in his reverence."

"Holy smoke! but you're gettin' desperate independent," said the Captain; "you had more than wan refreshment with him the day already," and the mate, admitting it remorsefully, relapsed into gloomy silence as they loitered about the Fair-ground.

"Peter," he said in a little, "did you ever try your fortune?"

"I never tried anything else," said the Captain; "but it's like the herrin' in Loch Fyne the noo — it's no' in't."

"That's no' what I mean," said Dougie; "there's a cluver woman roond in a cairt yonder, workin' wi' cairds and tea leaves and studyin' the palm o' the hand, and she'll tell you everything that happened past and future. I gave her a caal mysel' the noo, and she told me things that wass most astonishin'."

"What did it cost you?" asked Para Handy, with his interest immediately aroused.

"Ninepence."

"Holy smoke! she would need to be most extraordinar' astonishin' for ninepence; look at the chap in Archer's circus tying himself in knots for front sates threepence! Forbye, I don't believe in them spae-wifes; half the time they're only tellin' lies."

"This wan's right enough, I'll warrant you," said the mate; "she told me at once I wass a sailor and came through a lot of trouble."

"What did she predict? — that's the point, Dougie; they're no' mich use unless they can predict; I could tell myself by the look o' you that you had a lot o' trouble, the thing's quite common."

"No, no," said the mate cautiously; "pay ninepence for yoursel' if you want her to predict. She told me some eye-openers."

The Captain, with a passion for eye-openers, demanded to be led to the fortune-teller, and submitted himself to ninepence worth of divination, while Dougie waited outside on him. He, too, came forth, half elated, half depressed.

"What did she say to you?" asked the mate.

"She said I wass a sailor and seen a lot o' trouble," replied the Captain.

"Yes, but what did she predict?"

"Whatever it wass it cost me ninepence," said the Captain, "and I'm no' givin' away any birthday presents anymore than yoursel'; it's time we were back noo on the vessel."

Getting on board the *Vital Spark* at the quay they found that Para Handy's guess at the engineer's possession of something sensible in a bottle was correct. He hospitably passed it round, and was astonished to find the Captain and mate, for the first time in his experience, refuse a drink. They not only refused but were nasty about it.

"A' richt," he said; "there'll be a' the mair in the morn for me an' Jim. I daursay ye ken best yersel's when ye've gane ower faur wi't. I aye believe, mysel', in moderation."

The manner of Para Handy and his mate for a week after this was so peculiar as to be the subject of unending speculation on the part of the engineer and Sunny Jim. The most obvious feature of it was that they both regarded the engineer with suspicion and animosity.

"I'm shair I never did them ony hairm," he protested to Sunny Jim, almost in tears; "I never get a ceevil word frae either o' them.

Dougie's that doon on me, he wad raither gang withoot a smoke than ask a match affme."

"It's cruel, that's whit it is!" said Sunny Jim, who had a feeling heart; "but they're aff the dot ever since the nicht we were at Tarbert. Neither o' them'll eat fish, nor gang ashore efter it's dark. They baith took to their beds on Monday and wouldna steer oot o' their bunks a' day, pretendin' to be ill, but wonderfu' sherp in the appetite."

"I'll give them wan chance, and if they refuse it I'll wash my hands o' them," said Macphail decisively, and that evening after tea he produced a half-crown and extended a general invitation to the nearest tavern.

"Much obleeged, but I'm not in the need of anything," said the Captain. "Maybe Dougie —"

"No thanky," said the mate with equal emphasis; "I had a dram this week already" — a remark so ridiculous that it left the engineer speechless. He tapped his head significantly with a look at Sunny Jim, and the two of them went ashore to dispose of the half-crown without the desired assistance.

Next day there was an auction sale in the village, and Para Handy and his mate, without consulting each other, found themselves among the bidders.

"Were you fancyin' anything parteecular?" asked the Captain, who plainly had an interest in a battered old eight-day clock.

"No, nothing to mention," said the mate, with an eye likewise on the clock. "There's capital bargains here, I see, in crockery."

But the Captain seemed to have no need for crockery; he hung about an hour or two till the clock was put to the hammer, and offered fifteen shillings, thus completely discouraging a few of the natives who had concealed the hands and weights of the clock, and hoped to secure the article at the reasonable figure of about a crown. To the Captain's surprise and annoyance, he found his mate his only competitor, and between them they raised the price to thirty shillings, at which figure it was knocked down to the Captain, who had it promptly placed on a barrow and wheeled down to the quay.

"Were you desperate needin' a clock?" asked the mate, coming after him.

"I wass on the look-out for a clock like that for years," said the Captain, apparently charmed with his possession.

"I'll give you five-and-thirty shillings for't," said the mate, but Para Handy wasn't selling. He had the clock on board, and spent at least an hour investigating its interior, with results that from his aspect seemed thoroughly disappointing. He approached Dougie and informed him that he had changed his mind, and was willing to hand over the clock for five-and-thirty shillings. The bargain was eagerly seized by Dougie, who paid the money and submitted his purchase to an examination even more exhaustive than the Captain.

Half an hour later the engineer and Sunny Jim had to separate the Captain and the mate, who were at each other's throats, the latter frantically demanding back his money or a share of whatever the former had found inside the clock.

"The man's daft," protested Para Handy; "the only thing that was in the clock wass the works and an empty bottle."

"The Tarbert spae-wife said I would find a fortune in a clock like that," spluttered Dougie.

"Holy smoke! She said the same to me," confessed the Captain. "And did she say that eatin' fish wass dangerous?"

"She did that," said the mate. "Did she tell you to keep your bed on the first o' the month in case o' accidents?"

"Her very words!" said the Captain. "Did she tell you to beware o' a man wi' black whiskers that came from Australia?" and he looked at the engineer.

"She told me he was my bitterest enemy," said the mate.

"And that's the way ye had the pick at me!" exclaimed the engineer. "Ye're a couple o' Hielan' cuddies; man, I never wass nearer Australia than the River Plate."

On the following day a clock went cheap at the head of the quay for fifteen shillings, and the loss was amicably shared by Para Handy and his mate, but any allusion to Tarbert Fair and fortune-telling has ever since been bitterly resented by them both.

THE HAIR LOTION

*D*ougie, the mate, had so long referred to his family album as a proof of the real existence of old friends regarding whom he had marvelous stories to tell, that the crew finally demanded its production. He protested that it would be difficult to get it out of the house, as his wife had it fair in the middle of the parlor table, on top of the Family Bible.

"Ye can ask her for the len' o't, surely," said the Captain. "There's nobody goin' to pawn it on her. Tell her it's to show your shup-mates what a tipper she wass hersel' when she wass in her prime."

"She's in her prime yet," said the mate, with some annoyance.

"Chust that!" said Para Handy. "A handsome gyurl, I'm sure of it; but every woman thinks she wass at her best before her husband mairried her. Let you on that you were bouncin' aboot her beauty, and tell her the enchineer wass dubious —"

"Don't drag me into't," said the engineer. "You micht hae married Lily Langtry for a' I care; put the blame on the Captain; he's what they ca' a connysure among the girls," a statement on which the Captain darkly brooded for several days after.

The mate ultimately rose to the occasion, and taking advantage of a visit by his wife to her good-sister, came on board one day with the album wrapped in his oilskin trousers. It created the greatest interest on the *Vital Spark,* and an admiration only marred by the discovery that the owner was attempting to pass off a lithograph portrait of the late John Bright as that of his Uncle Sandy.

"My mistake!" he said politely, when the engineer corrected him; "I thocht it wass Uncle Sandy by the whuskers; when I look again I see he hasna the breadth across the shouthers."

"Wha's this chap like a body-snatcher?" asked the engineer, turning over another page of the album. "If I had a face like that I wad try and no' keep mind o't."

"You're a body-snatcher yoursel'," said the mate warmly, "and that's my advice to you. Buy specs, Macphail; you're spoilin' your eyes wi' readin' them novelles."

"Holy smoke!" cried the Captain; "it's a picture o'yoursel', Dougie. Man! what a heid o'hair!"

"I had a fair quantity," said the mate, passing his hand sadly over a skull which was now as bare as a bollard. "I'm sure I don't ken what way I lost it."

"Short bunks for sleepin' in," suggested the Captain kindly; "that's the worst o' bein' a sailor."

"I tried everything, from paraffin oil to pumice-stone, but nothing did a bit of good; it came oot in handfuls."

"I wad hae left her," said the engineer. "When a wife tak's her hands to ye the law says ye can leave her and tak' the weans wi' ye."

"I see ye hae been consultin' the lawyers," retorted the mate readily; "what way's your ear keepin' efter your last argument wi' the flet-iron?" and Macphail retired in dudgeon to his engines.

Sunny Jim regarded Dougie's portrait thoughtfully. "Man!" he said, "if the Petroloid Lotion had been invented in them days ye could hae had your hair yet. That's the stuff! Fair champion! Rub it on the doorstep and ye didna need to keep a bass. The hair mak's a difference, richt enough; your face is jist the same's it used to be, but the hair in the photo mak's ye twenty years younger. It's as nice a photo as ever I seed; there's money in't."

"None o' your dydoes noo!" said the mate, remembering how Sunny Jim had found money in the exploitation of the Tobermory whale. "If you think I would make an exhibeetion o' my photygraph —"

"Exhibeetion my aunty!" exclaimed Sunny Jim. "Ye're no' an Edna May. But I'll tell ye whit we could dae. Thae Petroloid Lotion folks is keen on testimonials. A' ye hae to dae is to get Macphail to write a line for ye saying ye lost yer hair in a biler explosion, and tried Petroloid, and it brocht it back in a couple o' weeks. Get a photograph o' yersel' the way ye are the noo and send it, and this yin wi' the testimonial, lettin' on the new yin's the way ye looked immediately efter the explosion, and this yin's the way ye look since ye took to usin' the lotion."

"Capital!" cried the Captain, slapping his knees. "For ingenuity you're chust sublime, Jum."

"Sublime enough," said Dougie cautiously, "but I thocht you said there wass money in it."

"So there is," said Sunny Jim. "The Petroloid Lotion folk'll gie ye a pound or twa for the testimonial; I kent a chap that made his livin' oot o' curin' himsel' o' diseases he never had, wi' pills he never saw except in pictures. He was a fair don at desoribin' a buzzin' in the ear, a dizzy heid, or a pain alang the spine o' his back, and was dragged back frae the brink o' the grave a thoosand times, by his way o't, under a different name every time. Macphail couldna touch him at a testimonial for anything internal, but there's naething to hinder Macphail puttin' a bit thegither aboot the loss and restoration o' Dougie's hair. Are ye game, Dougie?"

The mate consented dubiously, and the engineer was called upon to indite the requisite document, which took him a couple of evenings, on one of which the mate was taken ashore at Rothesay and photographed in the Captain's best blue pilot pea-jacket. The portraits and the testimonial were duly sent to the address which was found in the advertisement of Petroloid's Lotion for the Hair, a gentle hint being included that some "recognition" would be looked for, the phrase being Sunny Jim's. Then the crew of the

Vital Spark resigned themselves to a patient wait of several days for an acknowledgment.

Three weeks passed, and Sunny Jim's scheme was sadly confessed a failure, for nothing happened, and the cost of the Rothesay photograph, which had been jointly borne by the crew on the understanding that they were to share alike in the products of it, was a subject of frequent and unfeeling remarks from the engineer, who suggested that the mate had got a remittance and said nothing about it. But one afternoon the Captain picked up a newspaper, and turning, as was his wont, to the pictorial part of it, gave an exclamation on beholding the two portraits of his mate side by side in the midst of a Petroloid advertisement.

"Holy smoke! Dougie," he cried, "here you are ass large ass life like a futbaal player or a man on his trial for manslaughter."

"Michty! iss that me?" said the mate incredulously. "I had no notion they would put me in the papers. If I kent that I would never have gone in for the ploy."

"Ye look guilty," said the engineer, scrutinising the blurred lineaments of his shipmate in the newspaper. "Which is the explosion yin? The testimonial's a' richt onyway; it's fine," and he read his own composition with complete approval —

I unfortunately lost all my hair in a boiler explosion, and tried all the doctors, but none of them could bring it back. Then I heard of your wonderful Petroloid Lotion, and got a small bottle, which I rubbed in night and morning as described. In a week there was a distinct improvement. In a fortnight I had to have my head shorn twice, and now it is as thick as ever it was. I will recommend your Lotion to all my friends, and you are at liberty to make any use of this you like. — (Signed) Dougald Campbell, Captain, *Vital Spark,*

"What's that?" cried Para Handy, jumping up. "Captain! who said he was captain?"

"The advertisement," said the engineer guiltily. "I never wrote 'captain'; they've gone and shifted a lot o' things I wrote, and spiled the grammar and spellin'. Fancy the way they spell distinck!"

A few days later a box was delivered on the *Vital Spark* which at first was fondly supposed to be a case of whisky lost by somebody's mistake, but was found on examination to be directed to the mate. It was opened eagerly, and revealed a couple of dozen of the Petroloid specific, with a letter containing the grateful acknowledgments of the manufacturers, and expressing a generous hope that as the lotion had done so much to restore their correspondent's hair, he would distribute the accompanying consignments among all his bald-headed friends.

"Jum," said the Captain sadly, "when you're in the trum for makin' money efter this, I'll advise you to tak' the thing in hand yoursel' and leave us oot of it."

PARA HANDY AND THE NAVY

*M*acphail the engineer sat on an upturned bucket reading the weekly paper, and full of patriotic alarm at the state of the British Navy.

"What are you groanin' and sniffin' at?" asked the Captain querulously. "I should think mysel' that by this time you would be tired o' Mrs. Atherton. Whatna prank iss she up to this time?"

"It's no' Mrs. Atherton," said the reader; "it's something mair important; it's the Germans."

"Holy smoke!" said Para Handy, "are they findin' them oot, noo? Wass I not convinced there wass something far, far wrong wi' them? Break the full parteeculars to me chently, Mac, and you, Jim, go and get the dinner ready; you're far too young to hear the truth aboot the Chermans. Which o' the Chermans iss it, Mac? Some wan in a good poseetion, I'll be bound! It's a mercy that we're sailors; you'll no' find mich aboot the wickedness o' sailors in the papers."

"The British Navy's a' to bleezes!" said Macphail emphatically. "Here's Germany buildin' Dreadnaught men-o'-war as hard's she can, and us palaverin' awa' oor time."

Para Handy looked a little disappointed. "It's politics you're on," said he; "and I wass thinkin' it wass maybe another aawful scandal in Society. That's the worst o' the newspapers — you never know where you are wi' them; a week ago it wass nothing but the high jeenks of the beauteous Mrs. Atherton. Do you tell me the Brutish Navy's railly done?"

"Complete!" said the engineer,

"Weel, that's a peety!" said Para Handy sympathetically; "it'll put a lot o' smert young fellows oot o' jobs; I know a Tarbert man called Colin Kerr that had a good poseetion on the Formidable. I'm aawful sorry aboot Colin."

The engineer resumed his paper, and the *Vital Spark* chug-chugged her sluggish way between the Gantocks and the Cloch, with Dougie at the wheel, his nether garments hung precariously on the half of a pair of braces. "There's nothing but dull tred everywhere," said he. "They're stoppin' a lot o' the railway steamers, too."

"The state o' the British Navy's mair important than the stoppage o' a wheen passenger steamers," explained the engineer. "If you chaps read the papers ye would see this country's in a bad poseetion. We used to rule the sea —"

"We did that!" said the Captain heartily; "I've seen us doin' it! Brutain's hardy sons!"

"And noo the Germans is gettin' the upper hand o' us; they'll soon hae faur mair Dreadnaughts than we hae. We're only buildin' four. Fancy that! Four Dreadnaughts at a time like this, wi' nae work on the Clyde, and us wi' that few Territorials we hae to go to the fitba' matches and haul them oot to jine by the hair o' the heid. We've lost the two-Power standard."

"Man, it's chust desperate!" said the Captain. "We'll likely advertise for't. What's the — what's the specialty aboot the Dreadnaughts?"

"It's the only cless o' man-o'-war that's coonted noo," said the engineer; "a tip-top battle-winner. If ye havena Dreadnaughts ye micht as weel hae dredgers."

"Holy smoke! what a lot o' lumber aal the other men-o'-war must be!" remarked the Captain. "That'll be the way they're givin' them up and payin' off the hands."

"Wha said they were givin' them up?" asked the engineer snappishly.

"Beg pardon! beg pardon! I thocht I heard you mention it yon time I remarked on Colin Kerr. I thocht that maybe aal the other boats wass absolute, and we would see them next week lyin' in the Kyles o' Bute wi' washin's hung oot on them."

"There's gaun to be nae obsolete boats in the British Navy efter this," said the engineer; "we're needin' every man-o'-war that'll baud thegither. The Germans has their eye on us."

"Dougie," said the Captain firmly, with a glance at the déshabillé of his mate, "go doon this instant and put on your jecket! The way you are, you're not a credit to the boat."

A terrific bang broke upon the silence of the Firth; the crew of the *Vital Spark* turned their gaze with one accord towards the neighborhood of Kilcreggan, whence the report seemed to have proceeded, and were frightfully alarmed a second or two afterwards when a shell burst on the surface of the sea a few hundred yards or so from them, throwing an enormous column of water into the air.

"What did I tell ye!" cried Macphail, as he dived below to his engine-room.

"Holy smoke!" exclaimed Para Handy; "did ye notice anything, Dougie?"

"I think I did!" said the mate, considerably perturbed; "there must be some wan blastin'."

"Yon wassna a blast," said the Captain; "they're firin' cannons at us from Portkill."

"There's a pant for ye!" exclaimed Sunny Jim, dodging behind the funnel.

"What for would they be firin' cannons at us?" asked the mate, with a ludicrous feeling that even the jacket advised a minute or two ago by the Captain would now be a most desirable protection.

Another explosion from the fort at Portkill postponed the Captain's answer, and this time the bursting shell seemed a little closer.

"Jim," said the mate appealingly, "would ye mind takin' baud o' this wheel till I go down below and get my jacket? If I'm to be shot, I'll be shot like a Hielan' chentleman and no' in my shirt-sleeves."

"You'll stay where you are!" exclaimed the Captain, greatly excited; "you'll stay where you are, and die at your post like a Brutish sailor. This iss *war*. Port her heid in for Macinroy's Point, Dougald, and you, Macphail, put on to her every pound of steam she'll cairry. I wish to Providence I had chust the wan wee Union Jeck."

"Whit would ye dae wi' a Union Jeck?" asked the engineer, putting up his head and ducking nervously as another shot boomed over the Firth.

"I would nail it to the mast!" said Para Handy, buttoning his coat. "It would show them Cherman chentlemen we're the reg'lar he'rts of oak."

"Ye don't think it's Germans that's firin', dae ye?" asked the engineer, cautiously putting out his head again. "It's the Garrison Arteelery that's firin' frae Portkill."

"Whit are the silly duvvles firin' at us for, then?" asked Para Handy; "I'm sure we never did them any herm."

"I ken whit for they're firin'," said the engineer maliciously; "they're takin' the *Vital Spark* for yin o' them German Dreadnaughts. Ye have nae idea o' the fear o' daith that's on the country since it lost the two-Power standard."

This notion greatly charmed the Captain, being distinctly complimentary to his vessel; but his vanity was soon dispelled, for Sunny Jim pointed out that the last shot had fallen far behind them, in proximity to a floating target now for the first time seen. "They're jist at big-gun practice," he remarked with some relief, "and we're oot o' the line o' fire."

"Of course we are!" said Para Handy. "I kent that aal along. Man, Macphail, but you were tumid, tumid! You're losin' aal your nerve wi' readin' aboot the Chermans."

PIRACY IN THE KYLES

"*I*'m goin' doon below to put on my shippers," said the Captain, as the vessel puffed her leisured way round Buttock Point; "keep your eye on the Collingwood, an' no' run into her; it would terribly vex the Admirality."

The mate, with a spoke of the wheel in the small of his back, and his hands in his trousers pockets, looked along the Kyles towards Colintraive, and remarked that he wasn't altogether blind.

"I didna say you were," said the Captain; "I wass chust advisin' caaution. You canna be too caautious, and if anything would happen it's mysel' would be the man responsible. Keep her heid a point away, an' no' be fallin' asleep till I get my sluppers on; you'll mind you were up last night pretty late in Tarbert."

Macphail, the engineer, projected a perspiring head from his engine-room, and wiped his brow with a wad of oily waste. "Whit's the argyment?" he asked. "Is this a coal-boat or a Convention o' Royal Burghs? I'm in the middle o' a fine story in the 'People's Frien',' and I canna hear mysel' readin' for you chaps barkin' at each other. I wish ye would talk wee."

Para Handy looked at him with a contemptuous eye, turned his back on him, and confined his address to Dougie. "I'll never feel safe in the Kyles of Bute," he said, "till them men-o'-war iss oot o' here. I'm feared for a collusion."

"There's no' much chance of a collusion wi' a boat like that," said the mate, with a glance at the great sheer hulk of the discarded man-o'-war.

"You would wonder!" said Para Handy. "I haf seen a smert enough sailor before now come into a collusion wi' the whole o' Cowal. And he wassna tryin't either! Keep her off yet, Dougald."

With his slippers substituted for his sea-boots, the Captain returned on deck, when the Collingwood was safely left astern; and, looking back, watched a couple of fishermen culling mussels off the lower plates of the obsolete ship of war. "They're a different cless of men aboot the Kyles from what there used to be," said he, "or it wouldn't be only bait they would be liftin' off a boat like that. If she wass there when Hurricane Jeck wass in his prime, he would have the very cannons off her, sellin' them for junk in Greenock.

"There's no' that hardy Brutish spirit in the boys that wass in't when Hurricane Jeck and me wags on the Aggie."

"Tell us the baur," pleaded Sunny Jim, seated on an upturned bucket, peeling the day's potatoes.

"It's not the only baur I could tell you about the same chentleman," said the Captain, "but it's wan that shows you his remarkable agility. Gie me a baud o' that wheel, Dougie; I may ass well be restin' my back ass you, and me the skipper. To let you ken, Jum, Hurricane Jeck wass a perfect chentleman, six feet two, ass broad in the back ass a shippin'-box, and the very duvvle for contrivance. He wass a man that wass namely in the clipper tred to China, and the Board o' Tred had never a hand on him; his navigation wass complete. You know that, Dougie, don't you?"

"Whatever you say yoursel'," replied the mate agreeably, cutting himself a generous plug of navy-blue tobacco. "I have nothing to say against the chap — except that he came from Campbeltown."

"He sailed wi' me for three or four years on the Aggie," said the Captain, "and a nicer man on a boat you wouldna meet, if you didna contradict him-There wass nothing at aal against his moral character, except that he always shaved himsel' on Sunday, whether he wass needin' it or no'. And a duvvle for recreation! Six feet three, if he wass an inch, and a back like a shippin'-box!"

"Where does the British spirit come in?" inquired the engineer, who was forced to relinquish his story and join his mates.

"Hold you on, and I'll tell you that," said Para Handy. "We were lyin' wan winter night at Tighnabruaich wi' a cargo o' stones for a place they call Glen Caladh, that wass buildin' at the time, and we wanted a bit o' rope for something in parteecular — I think it wass a bit of a net. There wass lyin' at Tighnabruaich at the time a nice wee steamer yat belonging to a chentleman in Gleska that was busy at his business, and nobody wass near her. 'We'll borrow a rope for the night from that nice wee yat,' said Hurricane Jeck, as smert as anything, and when it wass dark he took the punt and went off and came back wi' a rope that did the business. 'They havena much sense o' ropes that moored that boat in the Kyles,' said he; 'they had it flemished down and nate for liftin'. They must be naval architects.' The very next night did Jeck no' take the punt again and go oot to the wee steam-yat, and come back wi' a couple o' india-rubber basses and a weather-gless?"

"Holy smoke!" said Dougie. "Wasn't that chust desperate?"

"We were back at Tighnabruaich a week efter that," continued Para Handy, "and Jeck made some inquiries. Nobody had been near the wee steam-yat, though the name o' her in the Gaalic was the Eagle, and Jeck made oot it wass a special dispensation. 'The man that owned her must be deid,' said he, 'or he hasna his wuts aboot him; I'll take a turn aboard the night wi' a screw-driver, and see that all's in order.' He came back that night wi' a bag o' cleats, a binnacle, half a dozen handy blocks, two dozen o' empty bottles, and a quite good water-breaker.

"'They may call her the Eagle if they like,' says he, 'but I call her the Silver Mine. I wish they would put lights on her; I nearly broke my neck on the cabin stairs.'

"'Mind you, Jeck,' I says to him,' I don't ken anything aboot it. If you're no' comin' by aal them things honest, it'll give the Aggie a bad name.'

"'It's aal right, Peter,' says he, quite kind. 'Flotsam and jetsam; if you left them there, you don't ken who might lift them!' Oh, a smert, smert sailor, Jeck! Six feet four in his stockin's soles, and a back like a couple o' shippin'-boxes."

"He's gettin' on!" remarked the engineer sarcastically. "I'm gled I wasna his tailor."

"The Glen Caladh job kept us comin' and goin' aal winter," pursued the Captain, paying no attention. "Next week we were back again, and Jeck had a talk with the polisman at Tighnabruaich aboot the lower clesses. Jeck said the lower clesses up in Gleska were the worst you ever saw; they would rob the wheels off a railway train. The polisman said he could weel believe it, judgin' from the papers, but, thank the Lord! there wass only honest folk in the Kyles of Bute. 'It's aal right yet,' said Jeck to me that night; 'the man that owns the Silver Mine's in the Necropolis, and never said a word aboot the wee yat in his will.' In the mornin' I saw a clock, a couple o' North Sea charts, a trysail, a galley-stove, two kettles, and a nice decanter lyin' in the hold.

"'Jeck,' I says, 'is this a flittin'?"

"'I'll not deceive you, Peter,' he says, quite honest, 'it's a gift'; and he sold the lot on Setturday in Greenock."

"A man like that deserves thejyie," said the engineer indignantly.

"I wouldna caal it aalthegither fair horny," admitted the Captain, "parteeculariy as the rest of us never got more than a schooner o' beer or the like o't oot of it; but, man! you must admit the chap's agility! He cairried the business oot single-handed, and there wass few wass better able; he wass six feet six, and had a back on him like a Broomielaw shed. The next time we were in the Kyles, and he went off wi' the punt at night, he came back from the Silver Mine wi' her bowsprit, twenty faddom o' chain, two doors, and half a dozen port-holes."

"Oh, to bleezes!" exclaimed Sunny Jim incredulously, "noo you're coddin'! What wye could he steal her port-holes?"

"Quite easy!" said Para Handy. "I didna say he took the holes themsel's, but he twisted off the windows and the brass aboot them. You must mind the chap's agility! And that wassna the end of it, for next time the Aggie left the Kyles she had on board a beautiful vernished dinghy, a couple o' masts, no' bad, and a fine brass steam-yat funnel."

"Holy smoke!" said Dougie; "it's a wonder he didna strip the lead off her."

"He had it in his mind," exclaimed the Captain; "but, mind, he never consulted me aboot anything, and I only kent, as you might say, by accident, when he would be standin' me another schooner. It wass aalways a grief to Jeck that he didna take the boat the way she wass, and sail her where she would be properly appreciated. 'My mistake, chaps!' he would say; 'I might have kent they would miss the masts and funnel!'"

AMONG THE YACHTS

*M*acphail was stoking carefully and often, like a mother feeding her first baby; keeping his steam at the highest pressure short of blowing off the safety valve, on which he had tied a pig-iron bar; and driving the *Vital Spark* for all she was worth past Cowal. The lighter's bluff bows were high out of water, for she was empty, and she left a wake astern of her like a liner.

"She hass a capital turn of speed when you put her to it," said the Captain, quite delighted; "it's easy seen it's Setturday, and you're in a hurry to be home, Macphail. You're passin' roond that oil-can there the same ass if it wass a tea-pairty you were at, and nobody there but women. It's easy seen it wass a cargo of coals we had the last trip, and there's more in your bunkers than the owner paid for. But it's none o' my business; please yoursel'!"

"We'll easy be at Bowlin' before ten," said Dougie, consulting his watch. "You needna be so desperate anxious."

The engineer mopped himself fretfully with a fistful of oily waste and shrugged his shoulders. "If you chaps like to palaver awa' your time," said he, "it's all the same to me, but I was wantin' to see the end o' the racin'."

"Whatna racin'?" asked the Captain.

"Yat-racin'," said the engineer, with irony. "Ye'll maybe hae heard o't. If ye havena, ye should read the papers. There's a club they ca' the Royal Clyde at Hunter's Quay, and a couple o' boats they ca' the Shamrock and the White Heather are sailin' among a wheen o' ithers for a cup. I wouldna care if I saw the feenish; you chaps ncedna bother; just pull doon the slaps o' your keps on your e'en when ye pass them, and ye'll no' see onything."

"I don't see much in aal their yat-racin'," said Para Handy.

"If I was you, then, I would try the Eye Infirmary," retorted the engineer, "or wan o' them double-breisted spy-glesses. Yonder the boats; we're in lots o' time —" and he dived again among his engines, and they heard the hurried clatter of his shovel.

"Anything wi' Macphail for sport!" remarked the Captain sadly. "You would think at his time o' life, and the morn Sunday, that his meditaations would be different. . . . Give her a point to starboard, Dougie, and we'll tee them better. Vender's the Ma'oona; if the duvvle wass wise he would put aboot at wance or he'll hit that patch o' calm."

"There's an aawful money in them yats!" said the mate, who was at the wheel.

"I never could see the sense o't," remarked the Captain. . . . "There's the Hero tacking; man, she's smert! smert! Wan o' them Coats's boats; I wish she would win; I ken a chap that plays the pipes on her."

Dougie steered as close as he could on the racing cutters with a sportsman's scrupulous regard for wind and water. "What wan's that?" he asked, as they passed a thirty-rater which had struck the calm.

"That's the Pallas," said the Captain, who had a curiously copious knowledge of the craft he couldn't see the sense of. "Another wan o' the Coats's; every other wan you see belongs to Paisley. They buy them by the gross, the same ass they were pims, and distribute them every noo and then among the faimely. If you're a Coats you lose a lot o' time makin' up your mind what boat you'll sail tomorrow; the whole o' the Clyde below the Tail o' the Bank is chock-a-block wi' steamboat-yats and cutters the Coats's canna hail a boat ashore from to get a sail, for they canna mind their names. Still-and-on, there's nothing wrong wi' them — tip-top aportin' chentlcmen!"

"I sometimes wish, mysel', I had taken to the yats," said Dougie; "it's a suit or two o' clothes in the year, and a pleasant occupaation. Most o' the time in canvas shippers."

"You're better the way you are," said Para Handy; "there's nothing bates the mercantile marine for makin' sailors. Brutain's hardy sons! We could do withoot yats, but where would we be withoot oor coal-boats? Look at them chaps sprauchlin' on the deck; if they saw themsel's they would see they want another fut on that main-sheet. I wass a season or two in the yats mysel' — the good old Marjory. No' a bad job at aal, but aawful hurried. Holy smoke! the way they kept you jumpin' here and there the time she would be racin'! I would chust as soon be in a lawyer's office. If you stopped to draw your breath a minute you got yon across the ear from a swingin' boom. It's a special breed o' sailor-men you need for racin'-yats, and the worst you'll get iss off the Islands."

"It's a cleaner job at any rate than carryin' coals," remarked the mate, with an envious eye on the spotless decks of a heeling twenty-tonner.

"Clean enough, I'll alloo, and that's the worst of it," said Para Handy. "You might ass wcel be a chamber-maid — up in the momin' scourin' brass and scrubbin' floors, and goin' ashore wi' a fancy can for sixpenceworth o' milk and a dozen o' syphon soda. Not much navigation there, my lad!. . .If I wass that fellow I would gybe her there and set my spinnaker to starboard; what do you think yoursel', Macphail?"

"I thocht you werena interested," said the engineer, who had now reduced his speed.

"I'm not much interested, but I'm duvellish keen," said Para Handy. "Keep her goin' chust like that, Macphail; we'll soon be up wi' the Shamrock and the Heather; they're yonder off Loch Long."

A motor-boat regatta was going on at Dunoon; the *Vital Spark* seemed hardly to be moving as some of the competitors flashed past her, breathing petrol fumes.

"You canna do anything like that," said Dougie to the engineer, who snorted.

"No," said Macphail contemptuously, "I'm an engineer; I never was much o' a hand at the sewin'-machine. I couldna lower mysel' to handle engines ye could put in your waistcoat pocket."

"Whether you could or no'," said Para Handy, "the times iss changin', and the motor-launch iss coming for to stop."

"That's whit she's aye daein'," retorted the engineer; "stoppin's her strong p'int; gie me a good substantial compound engine; nane o' your hurdy-gurdies! I wish the wind would fresh a bit, for there's the Shamrock, and her mainsail shakin'." He dived below, and the *Vital Spark* in a little had her speed reduced to a crawl that kept her just abreast of the drifting racers.

"Paddy's hurricane — up and doon the mast," said Dougie in a tone of disappointment. "I would like, mysel', to see Sir Thomas Lipton winnin', for it's there I get my tea."

Para Handy extracted a gully-knife from the depths of his trousers pockets, opened it, spat on the blade for luck, and, walking forward, stuck it in the mast, where he left it. "That's the way to get wind," said he; "many a time I tried it, and it never fails. Stop you, and you'll see a breeze immediately. Them English skippers, Sycamore and Bevis, havena the heid to think o't."

"Whit's the use o' hangin' on here?" said the engineer, with a wink at Dougie; "it's time we were up the river; I'll better get her under weigh again."

The Captain turned on him with a flashing eye. "You'll do nothing o' the kind, Macphail," said he; "we'll stand by here and watch the feenish, if it's anytime before the Gleska Fair."

Shamrock, having split tacks off Kilcreggan, laid away to the west, while White Heather stood in for the Holy Loch, seeking the evening breeze that is apt to blow from the setting sun. It was the crisis of the day, and the crew of the *Vital Spark* watched speechlessly for a while the yachts manoeuvring. For an hour the cutter drifted on this starboard leg, and Sunny Jim, for reasons of his own, postponed the tea.

"It wants more knifes," said Para Handy; "have you wan, Dougie?" but Dougie had lost his pocket-knife a week ago, and the engineer had none either.

"If stickin' knifes in the mast would raise the wind," said Sunny Jim, "there would be gales by this time, for I stuck the tea-knife in an oor ago."

"Never kent it to fail afore!" said Para Handy. . . . "By George! it's comin'. Yonder's Bevis staying!"

White Heather, catching the wind, reached for the closing lap of the race with a bone in her mouth, and Para Handy watched her, fascinated, twisting the buttons off his waistcoat in his intense excitement. With a turn or two of the wheel the mate put the *Vital Spark* about and headed for the mark; Macphail deserted his engine and ran forward to the bow.

"The Heather hass it, Dougald," said the Captain thankfully; "I'm vexed for you, considerin' the place you get your tea."

"Hold you on, Peter," said the mate; "there's the Shamrock fetchin'; a race is no' done till it's feenished." His hopes were justified. Shamrock, only a few lengths behind, got the same light puff of wind in her sails, and rattled home a winner by half a minute.

"Macphail!" bawled the Captain, "I'll be much obleeged if you take your place again at your bits of engines, and get under weigh; it's any excuse wi' you for a diversion, and it's time we werena here."

FOG

*I*n a silver-grey fog that was not unpleasant, the *Vital Spark* lay at Tarbert quay, and Dougie read a belated evening paper.

"Desperate fog on the Clyde!" he said to his shipmates; "we're the lucky chaps that's here and oot o't! It hasna lifted in Gleska for two days, and there's any amount o' boats amissin' between the Broomielaw and Bowlin'."

"Tck! tck! issn't that deplorable?" said the Captain. "Efter you wi' the paper, Dougald. It must be full o' accidents."

"The Campbeltown boat iss lost since Setturday, and they're lookin' for her wi' lanterns up and doon the river. I hope she hassna many passengers; the poor sowls'll be stervin'."

"Duvvle the fear!" said Para Handy; "not on the Campbeltown boat ass long ass she has her usual cargo. I would sooner be lost wi' a cargo o' Campbeltown for a week than spend a month in wan o' them hydropathics."

"Two sailors went ashore at Bowlin' from the Benmore, and they havena been heard of since," proceeded the mate; "they couldna find their way back to the ship."

"And what happened then?" asked Para Handy.

"Nothing," replied the mate. "That's all; they couldna find their way back."

"Holy smoke!" reflected Para Handy, with genuine surprise; "they're surely ill off for news in the papers nooadays; or they must have a poor opeenion o' sailor-mep. They'll be thinkin' they should aalways be teetotalers."

The Captain got the paper to read for himself a little later, and discovered that the missing Benmore men had not lost themselves in the orthodox sailor way, but were really victims of the fog, and his heart went out to them. "I've seen the same thing happen to mysel'," he remarked. "It wass the time that Hurricane Jeck and me wass on the Julia. There wass a fog come on us wan time there so thick you could almost cut it up and sell it for briquettes."

"Help!" exclaimed Macphail.

"Away, you, Macphail, and study your novelles; what way's Lady Fitzgerald gettin' on in the chapter you're at the noo? It's a wonder to me you're no' greetin'," retorted the Captain; and this allusion to the sentimental tears of the engineer sent him down, annoyed, among his engines.

"It wass a fog that lasted near a week, and we got into it on a Monday mornin' chust below the Cloch. We were makin' home for Gleska. We fastened up to the quay at Gourock, waitin' for a change, and the thing that vexed us most wass that Hurricane Jeck and me wass both invited for that very night to a smaal tea-party oot in Kelvinside."

"It's yoursel' wass stylish!" said the mate. "It must have been before you lost your money in the City Bank."

"It wassna style at aal, but a Cowal gyurl we knew that wass cook to a chentleman in Kelvinside, and him away on business in Liverpool," explained the Captain. "Hurricane Jeck wass in love wi' the gyurl at the time, and her name wass Bella. 'This fog'll last for a day or two,' said Jeck in the efternoon; 'it's apeety to lose the ploy at Bella's party.'

"'What would you propose, yoursel'?' I asked him, though I wass the skipper. I had aye a great opeenion o' Hurricane Jeck's agility.

"'What's to hinder us takin' the train to Gleska, and leavin' the Julia here?' said Jeck, ass smert ass anything. 'There's nobody goin' to run away wi' her.'

"Jeck and me took the train for Gleska, and left the enchineer — a chap Macnair — in full command o' the vessel. I never could trust a man o' the name o' Macnair from that day on.

"It wass a splendid perty, and Jeck wass chust sublime. I never partook in a finer perty — two or three hens, a pie the size o' a binnacle, and wine! — the wine was chust miraculous. Bella kept it comin' in in quantities. The coalman wass there, and the letter-carrier, and the man that came for the grocer's orders, and there wassna a gas in the hoose that wassna bleezin'. You could see that Hurricane Jeck had his he'rt on makin' everybody happy. It wass him that danced the hornpipe on the table, and mostly him that carried the piano doon the stair to the dinin'-room. He fastened a clothes-line aft on the legs o' her, laid doon a couple o' planks, and slided her. 'Tail on to the rope, my laads!' says he, 'and I'll go in front and steady her.' But the clothes-rope broke, and the piano landed on his back. He never had the least suspeecion, but cairried her doon the rest o' the stair himsel', and put her in poseetion. And efter a' oor bother there wass nobody could play. 'That's the worst o' them fore-and-aft pianos!' said Jeck, ass vexed ass anything; 'they're that much complicated!'

"We were chust in the middle o' the second supper, and Bella wass bringin' in cigars, when her maister opened the door wi' his chubb, and dandered in! There wassna a train for Liverpool on account o' the fog!"

"'What's this?' says he, and Bella nearly fainted.

"'It's Miss Maclachlan's birthday' — meanin' Bella — answered Jeck, ass nice ass possible. 'You're chust in the nick o' time,' and he wass goin' to introduce the chentleman, for Jeck wass a man that never forgot his mainners.

"'What's that piano doin' there? 'the chentleman asked, quite furious.

"'You may weel ask that,' said Jeck, 'for aal the use it iss, we would be better wi' a concertina,' and Bella had to laugh.

"'I've a good mind to send for the polls,' said her maister.

"'You needna bother,' said Bella; 'he's comin' anyway, ass soon ass he's off his bate and shifted oot o' his uniform,' and that wass the only intimation and invitation Hurricane Jeck ever got that Bella wass goin' to mairry Macrae the polisman.

"We spent three days in the fog in Gleska, and aal oor money," proceeded Para Handy, "and then, 'It's time we were back on the hooker,' said Hurricane Jeck; 'I can mind her name; it's the Julia.'

"'It's no' so much her name that bothers me,' says I; 'it's her latitude and longitude; where in aal the world did we leave her?'

"'Them pink wines!' said Jeck. 'That's the rock we split on, Peter! The fog would never have lasted aal this time if we had taken Brutish spirits.'

"It wass chust luck we found the half o' a railway ticket in Jeck's pocket, and it put us in mind that we left the boat at Gourock. We took the last train doon, and landed there wi' the fog ass bad ass ever; aye, worse! it wass that thick noo, it wassna briquettes you would make wi't, but marble nocks and mantelpieces.

"'We left the Julia chust fornenst this shippin'-box,' said Jeck, on Gourock quay, and, sure enough, there wass the boat below, and a handy ladder. Him and me went doon the ladder to the deck, and whustled on Macnair. He never paid the least attention.

"'He'll be in his bed,' said Jeck; 'gie me a ha'ad o' a bit o' marlin'.'

"We went doon below and found him sleepin' in the dark; Jeck took a bit' o' the marlin', and tied him hands and feet, and the two o' us went to bed, ass tired ass anything, wi' oor boots on. You never, never, never saw such fog!

"Jeck wass the first to waken in the mornin', and he struck a match.

"'Peter,' said he, quite solemn, when it went oot, 'have we a stove wi' the name Eureka printed on the door?

"'No, nor Myreeka,' says I; 'there's no' a door at aal on oor stove, and fine ye ken it!'

"He lay a while in the dark, sayin' nothing, and then he struck another match. 'Is Macnair red-heided, do you mind?' says he when the match went oot.

"'Ass black ass the ace o' spades!' says I.

"'That wass what wass runnin' in my own mind,' said Jeck; 'but I thocht I maybe wass mistaken. *We're in oor bed in the wrong boat!*'

"And we were! We lowsed the chap and told him right enough it wass oor mistake, and gave him two or three o' Bella's best cigars, and then we went ashore to look for the Julia. You never saw such fog! And it wass Friday mornin'.

"'Where's the Julia?' we asked the harbor-maister. 'Her!' says he; 'the enchineer got tired waitin' on ye, and got a couple o' quayheid chaps and went crawlin' up the river wi' the tide on We'nesday!'

"So Hurricane Jeck and me lost more than oorsel's in the fog; we lost oor jobs," concluded Para Handy. "Never put your trust in a man Macnair!"

Chapter VIII

CHRISTMAS ON THE 'VITAL SPARK'

*T*here was something, plainly, weighing on Dougie's mind; he let his tea get cold, and merely toyed with his kippered herring; at intervals he sighed — an unsailorlike proceeding which considerably annoyed the engineer, Macphail.

"Whit's the maitter wi' ye?" he querulously inquired. "Ye would think it was the Fast, to hear ye. Are ye ruein' your misspent life?"

"Never you mind Macphail," advised the Captain; "a chentleman should aalways hev respect for another chentleman in tribulation. What way's the mustress, Dougald?" He held a large tablespoonful of marmalade suspended in his hand, while he put the question with genuine solicitude; Dougie's wife was the very woman, he knew, to have something or other seriously wrong with her just when other folk were getting into a nice and jovial spirit for New Year.

"Oh, she's fine, thanky, Peter," said the mate; "there's nothing spashial wrong wi' her except, noo and then, the rheumatism."

"She should aalways keep a raw potato in her pocket," said Para Handy; "it's the only cure."

"She micht as weel keep a nutmeg-grater in her coal-bunker," remarked the engineer. "Whit wye can a raw potato cure the rheumatism?"

"It's the — it's the influence," explained Para Handy vaguely. "Look at them Vibrators! But you'll believe in nothing, Macphail, unless you read aboot it in wan o' them novelles; you're chust an unfidel!" Dougie sighed again, and the engineer, protesting that his meal had been spoiled for him by his shipmate's melancholy, hurriedly finished his fifth cup of tea and went on deck. There were no indications that it was Christmas Eve; two men standing on the quay were strictly sober. Crarae is still a place where they thoroughly celebrate the Old New Year after a first rehearsal with the statutory one.

"If you're not feelin' very brusk you should go to your bed, Dougie," remarked the Captain sympathetically. "The time to stop trouble iss before it starts."

"There's nothing wrong wi' me," the mate assured him sadly; "we're weel off, livin' on the fat o' the land, and some folk stervin'."

"We are that!" agreed Para Handy, helping himself to Dougie's second kipper. "Were you thinkin' of any wan parteecular?"

"Did you know a quarryman here by the name o' Col Maclachlan?" asked the mate, and Para Handy, having carefully reflected, confessed he didn't.

"Neither did I," said Dougie; "but he died a year ago and left a weedow yonder, and the only thing that's for her iss the poorshouse at Lochgilpheid."

"Holy smoke!" exclaimed the Captain; "isn't that chust desperate! If it wass a cargo of coals we had this trip, we might be givin' her a pickle, but she couldna make mich wi' a bag o' whinstones."

"They tell me she's goin' to start and walk tomorrow momin' to Lochgilpheid, and she's an old done woman. She says she would be affronted for to go in the Cygnet or the Minard, for everyone on board would ken she was goin' to the poorshouse."

"Oh, to the muschief!" said Para Handy; "Macphail wass right — a body might ass weel be at a funeral ass in your company, and it conu'n' on to the New Year!" He fled on deck from this doleful atmosphere in the fo'c'sle, but came down again in a minute or two. "I wass thinkin' to mysel'," he remarked with diffidence to the mate, "that if the poor old body would come wi' us, we could give her a lift to Ardrishaig; what do you say?"

"Whatever you say yoursel'," said the mate; "but we would need to be aawfu' careful o' her feelin's, and she wouldna like to come doon the quay unless it wass in the dark."

"We'll start at six o'clock, then," said the Captain, "if you'll go ashore the now and make arrangements, and you needna bother aboot her feelin's; we'll handle them like gless."

As an alternative to walking to the poorhouse, the sail to Loohgilphead by the *Vital Spark* was quite agreeable to the widow, who turned up at the quay in the morning quite alone, too proud even to take her neighbors into her confidence. Para Handy helped her on board and made her comfortable.

"You're goin' to get a splendid day!" he assured her cheerfully. "Dougie, iss it nearly time for oor cup o' tea?"

"It'll be ready in a meenute," said Dougie, with delightful promptness, and went down to rouse Sunny Jim.

"We aalways have a cup o' tea at six o'clock on the *Fital Spark,*" the Captain informed the widow, with a fluency that astonished even the engineer. "And an egg; sometimes two. Jum'll boil you an egg."

"I'm sure I'm an aawful bother to you!" protested the poor old widow feebly.

"Bother!" said Para Handy; "not the slightest! The tea's there anyway. And the eggs. Efter that we'll have oor breakfast."

"I'll be a terrible expense to you," said the unhappy widow; and Para Handy chuckled jovially.

"Expense! Nonsense, Mrs. Maclachlan! Everything's paid for here by the owners; we're allooed more tea and eggs and things than we can eat. I'll be thinkin' mysel' it's a sin the way we hev to throw them sometimes over the side" — at which astounding effort of the imagination Macphail retired among his engines and relieved his feelings by a noisy application of the coaling shovel.

"I have the money for my ticket," said the widow, fumbling nervously for her purse.

"Ticket!" said Para Handy, with magnificent alarm. "If the Board o' Tred heard o' us chergin' money for a passage in the *Fital Spark*, we would never hear the end o't; it would cost us oor certuficate."

The widow enjoyed her tea immensely, and Para Handy talked incessantly about everything and every place but Lochgilphead, while the *Vital Spark* chug-chugged on her fateful way down Loch Fyne to the poorhouse.

"Did you know my man?" the woman suddenly asked, in an interval which even Para Handy's wonderful eloquence couldn't fill up.

"Iss it Col Maclachlan?" he exclaimed. "Fine! me'm; fine! Col and me wass weel acquent; it wass that that made me take the liberty to ask you. There wass never a finer man in Argyllshire than poor Col — a regular chentleman! I mind o' him in the — in the quarry. So do you, Dougie, didn't you?"

"I mind o' him caapital!" said Dougie, without a moment's hesitation. "The last time I saw him he lent me half-a-croon, and I never had the chance to pay him't back."

"I think mysel', if I mind right, it wass five shullin's," suggested Para Handy, putting his hand in his trousers pocket, with a wink to his mate, and Dougie quickly corrected himself; it *was* five shillings, now that he thought of it. But having gone aside for a little and consulted the engineer and Sunny Jim, he came back and said it was really eight-and-sixpence.

"There wass other three-and-six I got the lend o' from him another time," he said; "I could show you the very place it happened, and I wass nearly forgettin' aal aboot it."

"My! ye're an awfu' leear!" said the engineer in a whisper as they stood aside.

"Maybe I am," agreed the mate; "but did you ever, ever, ever hear such a caapital one ass the Captain?"

Sunny Jim had no sooner got the dishes cleaned from this informal meal than Para Handy went to him and commanded a speedy preparation of the breakfast.

"Right-oh!" said Sunny Jim; "I'll be able to tak' a job as a chef in yin o' thae Cunarders efter this. But I've naething else than tea and eggs."

"Weel, boil them!" said the Captain. "Keep on boilin' them! Things never look so black to a woman when she can get a cup o' tea, and an egg or two'll no' go wrong wi' her. Efter that you'll maybe give us a tune on your melodeon — something nice and cheery, mind; none o' your laments; they're no' the thing at aal for a weedow woman goin' to the poorshouse."

It was a charming day; the sea was calm; the extraordinary high spirits of the crew of the *Vital Spark* appeared to be contagious, and the widow confessed she had never enjoyed a sail so much since the year she had gone with Col on a trip to Rothesay.

"It's five-and-thirty years ago, and I never wass there again," she added, just a little sadly.

"Faith, you should come wi' us to Ro'say," said the Captain genially, and then regretted it.

"I canna," said the poor old body; "I'll never see Ro'say again, for I'm goin' to Lochgilphead."

"And you couldna be goin' to a nicer place!" declared Para Handy. "Lochgilpheid's chust sublime! Dougie himsel''ll tell you!"

"Salubrious!" said the mate. "And forbye, it's that healthy!"

"There wass nothing wrong wi' Crarae," said the widow pathetically, and Sunny Jim came to the rescue with another pot of tea.

"Many a time I'll be thinking to mysel' yonder that if I had a little money bye me, I would spend the rest o' my days in Lochgilpheid," said Para Handy. "You never saw a cheerier place —"

"Crarae wass very cheery, too — in the summertime — when Col wass livin'," said the widow.

"Oh, but there's an aawful lot to see aboot Lochgilpheid; that's the place for Life!" said Para Handy. "And such nice walks; there's — there's the road to Kilmartin, and Argyll Street, full o' splendid shops; and the steamers comin' to Ardrishaig, and every night the mail goes bye to Crarae and Inveraray" — here his knowledge of Lochgilphead's charms began to fail him.

"I didna think it would be so nice ass that," said the widow, less dispiritedly. "I forgot aboot the mail; I'll aye be seem' it passin' to Crarae."

"Of course you will!" said Para Handy gaily; "that's a thing I wouldna miss, mysel'. And anytime you take the notion, you'll can take a drive in the mail to Crarae if the weather's suitable."

"I would like it fine!" said the widow; "but — but maybe they'll no' let me. You would hear — you would hear where I wass goin' in Lochgilpheid?"

"I never heard a word!" protested Para Handy. "That minds me — will you have another egg? Jum, boil another egg for Mrs. Maclachlan!"

"You hev been very kind," said the widow gratefully, as the *Vital Spark* came into Ardrishaig pier; "you couldna hev been kinder."

"I'm sorry you have to waalk to Lochgilpheid," said the Captain.

"Oh, I'm no' that old but I can manage the waalk," she answered; "I'm only seventy."

"Seventy!" said Para Handy, with genuine surprise; "I didna think you would be anything like seventy."

"I'll be seventy next Thursday," said the widow, and Para Handy whistled.

"And what in the world are you goin' to Lochgilpheid for? — the last place on God's earth, next to London. Efter Thursday next you'll can get your five shillin's a week in Crarae."

"Five shillin's a week in Crarae!" said the widow mournfully; "I hope I'll be ass weel off ass that when I get to heaven!"

"Then never mind aboot heaven the noo," said Para Handy, clapping her on the back; "go back to Crarae wi' the Minard, and you'll get your pension regular every week — five shillin's."

"My pension!" said the widow, with surprise. "Fancy me wi' a pension; I never wass in the Airmy."

"Did nobody ever tell you that you wass entitled to a pension when they knew you were needin't?" asked the Captain, and the widow bridled.

"Nobody knew that I wass needin' anything," she exclaimed; "I took good care o' that."

Late that evening Mrs. Maclachlan arrived at Crarae in the Minard Castle with a full knowledge for the first time of her glorious rights as an aged British citizen, and the balance of 8s. 6d. forced upon her by the mate, who had so opportunely remembered that he was due that sum to the lamented Col.

Chapter IX

THE MAIDS OF BUTE

*E*ven the captain of a steam lighter may feel the cheerful, exhilarating influence of spring, and Para Handy, sitting on an upturned pail, with his feet on a coil of rope, beiked himself in the sun and sang like a Untie — a rather croupy Untie. The song he sang was:

"Blow ye winds aye-oh!
 For it's roving I will go,
 I'll stay no more on England's shore,
 So let the music play.
 I'm off by the morning train,
 Across the raging main,
 I have booked a trup wi' a Government shup,
 Ten thousand miles away."

"Who's that greetin'?" asked the engineer maliciously, sticking his head out of the engine-room.

The Captain looked at him with contempt. "Nobody's greetin'," he said. "It's a thing you don't know anything at aal about; it's music. Away and read your novelles. What way's Lady Fitzgerald gettin' on wi' her new man?"

The engineer hastily withdrew.

"That's the way to settle him," said the Captain to Dougie and Sunny Jim. "Short and sweet! I could sing him blin'. Do ye know the way it iss that steamboat enchineers is aalways doon in the mooth like that? It's the want o' nature. They never let themselves go. Poor duvvils, workin' away among their bits o' enchines, they never get the wind and the sun aboot them right the same ass us seamen. If I wass always doon in a hole like that place o' Macphail's dabbin' my face wi' an oily rag aal day, I would maybe be ass ugly ass himsel'. Man, I'm feelin' fine! There's nothing like the spring o' the year, when you can get it like this. It's chust sublime! I'm feelin' ass strong ass a lion. I could pull the mast oot o' the boat and bate Brussels carpets wi' it."

"We'll pay for this yet," said Sunny Jim. "Ye'll see it'll rain or snow before night. What do ye say, Dougie?"

"Whatever ye think yoursel'," said Dougie.

"At this time o' the year," said the Captain, "I wish I wass back in MacBrayne's boats. The *Fital Spark* iss a splendid shup, the best in the tred, but there's no diversion. I wass the first man that ever pented the Maids o' Bute."

"Ye don't tell me!" exclaimed Dougie incredulously.

"I wass that," said Para Handy, as modestly as possible. "I'm not sayin' it for a bounce; the job might have come anybody's way, but I wass the man that got it. I wass a hand on the Inveraray Castle at the time. The Captain says to me wan day we were passin' the Maids — only they werena the Maids then; they hadna their clothes on — 'Peter, what do you think o' them two stones on the hull-side?'

"'They'll be there a long while before they're small enough to pap at birds wi,' says I.

"'But do they no' put ye desperate in mind o' a couple o' weemen?' said he.

"'Not them!' say I. 'I have been passin' here for fifteen years, and I never heard them taalkin' yet. If they were like weemen what would they be sittin' waitin' there for so long, and no' a man on the whole o' this side o' Bute?'

"'Aye, but it's the look o' them,' said the Captain. 'If ye stand here and shut wan eye, they'll put ye aawfu' in mind o' the two MacFadyen gyurls up in Penny-more. I think we'll chust christen them the Maids o' Bute.'

"Well, we aalways caaled them the Maids o' Bute efter that, and pointed them oot to aal the passengers on the steamers. Some o' them said they were desperate like weemen, and others said they were chust like two big stones. The Captain o' the Inveraray Castle got quite wild at some passengers that said they werena a bit like weemen. 'That's the worst o' them English towerists,' he would say. 'They have no imachination. I could make myself believe them two stones wass a regiment o' sodgers if I put my mind to't. I'm sure the towerists might streetch a point the same ass other folk, and keep up the amusement.'

"Wan day the skipper came to me and says, 'Are ye on for a nice holiday, Peter?' It wass chust this time o' the year and weather like this, and I wass feelin' fine.

"'No objections,' says I.

"'Well,' he says, 'I wish you would go off at Tighnabruaich and take some pent wi' ye in a small boat over to the Maids, and give them a touch o' rud and white that'll make them more like weemen than ever.'

"'I don't like,' said I.

"'What way do ye no' like?' said the skipper. 'It's no' even what you would caal work; it's chust amusement!'

"'But will it no' look droll for a sailor to be pentin' clothes on a couple o' stones, aal his lone by himsel' in the north end o' Bute, and no' a sowl to see him? Chust give it a think yersel', skipper; would it no' look awfu' daft?'

"'I don't care if it looks daft enough for the Lochgilphead Asylum, ye'll have to do it,' said the skipper. Til put ye off at Tighnabruaich this efternoon; ye can go over and do the chob, and take a night's ludgin's in the toon, and we'll pick you up tomorrow when we're comin' doon. See you and make the Maids as smert as ye can, and, by Chove, they'll give the towerists a start!'

"Weel, I wass put off at Tighnabruaich, and the rud and white pent wi' me. I got ludgin's, took my tea and a herrin' to't, and rowed mysel' over in a boat to Bute. Some of the boys aboot the quay wass askin' what I wass efter, but it wassna likely I would tell them I wass goin' to pent clothes on the Maids o'Bute; they would be sure to caal me the manta-maker efter it. So I chust said I wass going over to mark oot the place for a new quay MacBrayne wass buildin'. There's nothing like discretioncy.

"It wass a day that wass chust sublime! The watter wass that calm you could see your face in it, the birds were singing like hey-my-nanny, and the Kyles wass lovely. Two meenutes efter I started pentin' the Maids I wass singin' to mysel' like anything. Now I must let you ken I never had no education at drawin', and it's wonderful how fine I pented them. When you got close to them they were no more like rale maids than I am; ye wouldna take them for maids even in the dark, but before I wass done with them, ye would ask them up to dance. The only thing that vexed me wass that I had only the rud and white; if I had magenta and blue and yellow, and the like o' that, I could have made them far more stylish. I gave them white faces and rud frocks and bonnets, and man, man, it wass a splendid day!

"I took the notion in my heid that maybe the skipper o' the Inveraray wass right, and that they were maids at wan time, that looked back the same as Lot's wife in the Scruptures and got turned into stone. When I wassna singin', I would be speakin' away to them, and I'll assure ye it wass the first time maids never gave me any back chat. Wan o' them I called Mery efter — efter a gyurl I knew, and the other I called 'Lizabeth, for she chust looked like it. And it wass a majestic day. 'There ye are, gyurls,' I says to them,' and you never had clothes that fitted better. Stop you, and if I'm spared till next year, you'll have the magenta too.' The north end o' Bute iss a bleak, wild, lonely place, but when I wass done pentin' the Maids it looked like a lerge population. They looked that nate and cheery among the heather! Mery had a waist ye could get your arm roond, but 'Lizabeth wass a broad, broad gyurl. And I wassna a bad-lookin' chap mysel'."

Here Para Handy stopped and sighed.

"Go on wi' your baur," said Dougie.

"Old times! old times!" said the Captain. "By Chove! I wass in trum that day! I never saw finer weather, nor nicer gyurls. Och! but it wass chust imachination; when we pass the Maids o' Bute now, I know they're only stones, with rud and white pent on them. They're good enough for towerists."

Chapter X

HERRING — A GOSSIP

"Of aal the fish there iss in the sea," said Para Handy, "nothing bates the herrin'; it's a providence they're plentiful and them so cheap!"

"They're no' in Loch Fyne, wherever they are," said Dougie sadly; "the only herrin' that they're gettin' there iss rud ones comin' up in barrels wi' the Cygnet or the Minard Castle. For five years back the trade wass desperate."

"I wouldna say but you're right," agreeably remarked the Captain. "The herrin' iss a great, great mystery. The more you will be catchin' of them the more there iss; and when they're no' in't at aal they're no' there" — a great philosophic truth which the crew smoked over in silence for a few minutes.

"When I wass a hand on the gabberts," continued the Captain, "the herrin' fishin' of Loch Fyne wass in its prime. You ken yoursel' what I mean; if you don't believe me, Jum, there's Dougie himsel''ll tell you. Fortunes! chust simply fortunes! You couldna show your face in Tarbert then but a lot of the laads would gaither round at wance and make a jovial day of it. Wi' a barrel of nets in a skiff and a handy wife at the guttin', a man of the least agility could make enough in a month to build a land o' nooses, and the rale Loch Fyne was terrible namely over aal the world."

"I mind o't mysel'," said Sunny Jim; "they never sold onything else but the rale Loch Fyne in Gleska."

"They did that whether or no'," explained Para Handy, "for it wass the herrin's of Loch Fyne that had the reputation."

"I've seen the Rooshians eatin' them raw in the Baltic," said Macphail, the engineer, and Dougie shuddered. "Eating them raw!" said he; "the dirty duvvles!"

"The herrin' wass that thick in Loch Fyne in them days," recalled the Captain, "that you sometimes couldna get your anchor to the ground, and the quality was chust sublime. It wassna a tred at aal so much as an amusement; you went oot at night when the weans wass in their beds, and you had a couple o' cran on the road to Clyde in time for Gleska's breakfast. The quays wass covered wi' John O'Brian's boxes, and man alive! but the wine and spirit tred wass busy. Loch Fyne wass the place for Life in them days — high jeenks and big hauls; you werena very smert if you werena into both o' them. If you don't believe me, Dougie himsel''ll tell you."

"You have it exact, Peter," guaranteed the mate, who was thus appealed to; "I wass there mysel'."

"Of course I have it exact," said Para Handy; "I'll assure you it's no' a thing I read in the papers. Today there's no a herrin' in Loch Fyne or I'm mistaken."

"If there's wan he'll be kind o' lonely," said the mate. "I wonder what in the muschief's wrong wi' them?"

"You might shot miles o' nets for a month and there's no' a herrin' will come near them."

"Man! aren't they the tumid, frightened idiots!" said Dougie, with disgust.

"If ye ask me, I think whit spoiled the herrin' fishing in Loch Fyne was the way they gaed on writin' aboot it in the papers," said Macphail. "It was enough to scunner ony self-respectin' fish. Wan day a chap would write that it was the trawlers that were daein' a' the damage; next day anither chap would say he was a liar, and that trawlin' was a thing the herrin' thrived on. Then a chap would write that there should be a close time so as to gie the herrin' time to draw their breaths for anither breenge into the nets; and anither chap would write from Campbeltoon and say a close time would be takin' the bread oot o' the mooth o' his wife and weans. A scientific man said herrin' came on cycles —"

"He's a liar, anyway," said the Captain, with conviction. "They were in Loch Fyne afore the cycle was invented. Are you sure, Macphail, it's no' the cod he means?"

"He said the herrin' fishin' aye missed some years noo and then in a' the herrin' places in Europe as weel's in Loch Fyne, and the Gulf Stream had something to dae wi't."

"That's the worst o' science," said the Captain piously; "it takes aal the credit away from the Creator. Don't you pay attention to an unfidel like that; when the herrin' wass in Loch Fyne they stayed there aal the time, and only maybe took a daunder oot noo and then the length o' Ballantrae."

"If it's no' the Gulf Stream, then ye'll maybe tell us whit it is?" said the engineer, with some annoyance.

"I'll soon do that," said Para Handy; "if you want to ken, it's what I said — the herrin' iss a mystery, chust a mystery!"

"I'm awfu' gled ye told me," said the engineer ironically. "I aye wondered. Whit's the partcecular mysteriousness aboot it?"

"It's a silly fish," replied the Captain; "it's fine for eatin', but it hasna the sagacity. If it had the sagacity it wouldna come lower than Otter Ferry, nor be gallivantin' roond the Kyles o' Bute in daylight. It's them innovations that's the death o' herrin'. If the herrin' stayed in Loch Fyne attendin' to its business and givin' the drift-net crews encouragement, it would have a happier life and die respected.

"Whenever the herrin' of Loch Fyne puts his nose below Kilfinan, his character is gone. First the Tarbert trawlers take him oot to company and turn his heid; then there iss nothing for it for him but flying trips to the Kyles o' Bute, the Tail o' the Bank, and Gareloch. In Loch Fyne we never would touch the herrin' in the daytime, nor in winter; they need a rest, forbye we're none the worse o' one oorsel's; but the folk below Kilfinan have no regard for Christian principles, and they no sooner see an eye o' fish than they're roond aboot it with trawls, even if it's the middle o' the day or New Year's mornin'. They never give the fish a chance; they keep it on the run till its fins get hot. If it ventures ass far ass the Tail o' the Bank, it gets that dizzy wi' the sight o' the shippin' traffic that it loses the way and never comes back to Loch Fyne again. A silly fish! If it only had sagacity! Amn't I right, Dougie?"

"Whatever you say yoursel'. Captain; there's wan thing sure, the herrin's scarce."

"The long and the short of it iss that they're a mystery," concluded Para Handy.

Chapter XI

TO CAMPBELTOWN BY SEA

"Man, it's hot; most desperate hot!" said Para Handy, using his hand like a squeegee to remove the perspiration from his brow. "Life in weather like thiss iss a burden; a body might ass weel be burnin' lime or at the bakin'. I wish I wass a fush."

The *Vital Spark* was lying at Skipness, the tar boiling between her seams in unusually ardent weather, and Macphail on deck, with a horror of his own engine-room.

"Bein' a fush wouldna be bad," said Dougie, "if it wass not for the constant watter. The only thing you can say for waiter iss that it's wet and fine for sailin' boats on. If you were a fush, Captain, you would die of thirst."

"Walter, waiter everywhere, And not a single drop of drink," quoted the engineer, who was literary.

The Captain looked at him with some annoyance. "It's bad enough, Macphail," said he, "withoot you harpin', harpin' on the thing. You have no consuderation! I never mentioned drink. I wass thinkin' of us plowterin' doon in weather like this to Campbeltown, and wishin' I could swim."

"Can you no' swim?" asked Sunny Jim with some surprise.

"I daresay I could, but I never tried," said Para Handy. "I had never the time, havin' aye to attend to my business."

"Swimmin's aal the rage chust now," remarked Dougie, who occasionally read a newspaper. "Look at the Thames in London — there's men and women swimmin' it in droves; they'll do six or seven miles before their breakfast. And the Straits o' Dover's busy wi' splendid swimmers makin' their way to France."

"What are they wantin' to France for?" asked Para Handy. "Did they do anything?"

"I wouldna say," replied the mate; "it's like enough the polis iss after them, but the story they have themsel's iss that they're swimmin' for a wudger. The best this season iss a Gleska man caaled Wolfie; he swam that close to France the other day he could hear the natives taalkin'.""

"What for did he no' land?" asked Sunny Jim.

"I canna tell," said Dougie, "but it's likely it would be wan o' the places where they charge a penny at the quay. Him bein' a Gleska man, he would see them d — d first, so he chust came back to Dover."

"I don't see the fun of it, mysel'," said Para Handy reflectively. "But of course, if it's a wudger —"

"That's what I'm throng tellin' you," said the mate. "It looks a terrible task, but it's simple enough for any man with the agility. First you put off your clo'es and leave them in the shippin'-box at Dover if you have the confidence. Then you oil yoursel' wi' oil, put on a pair o' goggles, and get your photygraph. When the crood's big enough you kiss the wife good-bye and start swimmin' like anything."

"Whit wife?" asked the engineer, whose profound knowledge of life as depicted in penny novelettes had rendered him dubious of all adventures designed to end in France.

"Your own wife, of course," said Para Handy impatiently. "What other wife would a chap want to leave and go to France for? Go on wi' your story, Dougie."

"Three steamers loaded wi' beef-tea, champagne, chocolate, and pipers follows you aal the way —"

"Beef-tea and chocolate!" exclaimed the Captain, with astonishment. "What's the sense o' that? Are you sure it's beef-tea, Dougie?"

"I read it mysel' in the papers," the mate assured him. "You strike out aalways wi' a firm, powerful, overhand stroke, and whenever you're past the heid o' Dover quay you turn on your back, take your luncheon oot of a bottle, and tell the folk on the steamers that you're feelin' fine."

"You might well be feelin' fine, wi' a luncheon oot o' a bottle," said Para Handy. "It's the beef-tea that bothers me."

"Aal the time the pipers iss standin' on the paiddle-boxes o' the steamers playin' 'Hielan' Laddie' and 'The Campbells iss Comin'.'"

"Aal the time!" repeated Para Handy. "I don't believe wan word of it! Not aboot pipers; take my word for it, Dougie, they'll be doon below noo and then; there's nothing in this world thirstier than music."

"Do they no' get ony prizes for soomin' a' that distance?" asked Sunny Jim.

"I'll warrant you there must be money in it some way," said the engineer. "Whatever side they land on, they'll put roond the hat. There's naething the public'll pay you quicker or better for, than for daein' wi' your legs what an engine'll dae faur better."

"I could soom ony o' them blin'!" said Sunny Jim. "I was the natest wee soomer ever Geordie Geddes dragged by the hair o' the heid frae the Clyde at Jenny's Burn. Fair champion! Could we no' get up a soom frae here to Campbeltown the morn, and mak' a trifle at the start and feenish?"

"Man! you couldna swim aal that distance," said the Captain. "It would take you a week and a tug to tow you."

"I'm no' daft," explained Sunny Jim; "the hale thing's in the startin', for seemin'ly naebody ever feenishes soomin' ower to France. A' I hae to dae is to ile mysel' and dive, and the *Vital Spark* can keep me company into Kilbrannan Sound."

"There's the photygraphs, and the beef-tea, and the pipers," said the engineer; "unless ye hae them ye micht as well jist walk to Campbeltown."

"Dougie can play his trump, and that'll dae instead o' the pipers," said Sunny Jim. "It's a' in the start. See? I'll jump in at the quay, and you'll collect the money from the Skipness folk, and pick me up whenever they're oot o' sicht. I'll dae the dive again afore we come into Campbeltown, and Dougie'll baud the watch and gie a guarantee I swam the hale length o' Kintyre in four oors and five-and-twenty minutes. Then — bizz! — bang! — roon' the folk in Campbeltown wi' the bonny wee hat again! See?"

"Man! your cluvemess is chust sublime!" said Para Handy; "we'll have the demonstration in the mornin'."

The intelligence that the cook of the *Vital Spark* was to swim to Campbeltown found Skipness curiously indifferent. "If he had been swimming *from* Campbeltown it might be different," said the natives; so the attempts to collect a subscription in recognition of the gallant feat were poorly recognized and Sunny Jim, disgusted, quitted the water, and resumed his clothes on the deck of the vessel less than a hundred yards from the shore. The *Vital Spark* next day came into Campbeltown, and the intrepid swimmer, having quietly dropped over the side at not too great a distance, swam in the direction of the quay, at which he arrived with no demonstration of excitement on the part of the population.

"Swam aal the way from Skipness," Para Handy informed the curious; "we're raisin' a little money to encourage him; he's none of your Dover Frenchmen, but wan of Brutain's hardy sons. Whatever you think yoursel's in silver, chentlemen."

"Wass he in the waiter aal the time?" asked a native fisherman, copiously perspiring under a couple of guernseys and an enormous woolen comforter.

"He wass that!" Para Handy assured him. "If you don't believe me, Dougie himsel'"ll tell you."

"Then he wass the lucky chap!" said the native enviously. "It must have been fine and cool. What's he goin' to stand?"

Chapter XII

HOW TO BUY A BOAT

*I*t was shown in a former escapade of Para Handy's that he wasn't averse from a little sea-trout poaching. He justified this sport in Gaelic, always quoting a proverb that a switch from the forest, a bird from the hill, or a fish from the river were the natural right of every Highland gentleman. Sunny Jim approved the principle most heartily, and proposed to insert a clause including dogs, of which he confessed he had been a great admirer and collector in his Clutha days. Ostensibly the Captain never fished for anything but flounders, and his astonishment when he came on sea-trout or grilse in his net after an hour's assiduous plashing with it at the mouth of a burn was charming to witness.

"Holy smoke!" he would exclaim, scratching his ears, "here's a wheen o' the white fellows, and us chust desperate for cod. It's likely they're the Duke's or Mr. Younger's, and they lost their way to Bullingsgate. Stop you! Dougie, a meenute and hand me up a fut-spar. . . . I'm sure and I wassna wantin' them, but there they are, and what can you make of it? They might be saithe; it's desperate dark the night; what a peety we didna bring a lantern. Look and see if you divna think they're saithe, Dougie."

"Whatever you say yoursel'," was the mate's unvarying decision, and it could never be properly made out whether the fish were saithe or salmon till the crew had eaten them.

There was one favorite fishing bank of the Captain's inconveniently close to the county police station.

The constable was very apt to find a grilse on the inside handle of his coal-cellar door on mornings when the *Vital Spark* was in the harbor, and he, also, was much surprised, but never mentioned it, except in a roundabout way, to Para Handy.

"You must be makin' less noise oot in the bay at night," he would say to him. "By Chove! I could hear you mysel' last night quite plain; if you're not more caatious I'll have to display my activity and find a clue."

It was most unfortunate that the men of the *Vital Spark* should have come on a shoal of the "white fellows" one early morning when the river-watchers were in straits to justify their job. The lighter's punt, with an excellent net and its contents, had hurriedly to be abandoned, and before breakfast the Captain had lodged a charge of larceny against parties unknown at the police station. Someone had stolen his punt, he said, cutting the painter of her during the calm and virtuous sleep of self and mates. He identified the boat in the possession of the river-bailiffs; he was horrified to leam of the nefarious purpose to which it had been applied, but had to submit with curious equanimity to its confiscation. Local sympathy was aroused — fostered unostentatiously by the policeman; a subscription sheet was passed round the village philanthropists — also on the discreet suggestion of the policeman; and the sum of two pounds ten and ten-pence was collected — the tenpence being in ha'pence ingeniously abstracted by means of a table-knife from a tin bank in the possession of the policeman's only boy.

"You will go at wance to Tighnabruaich and buy yourself another boat, Peter," said the policeman, when informally handing over the money. "If you are circumspect and caautious you'll pick up a smert one chape that will serve for your requirements."

"I wouldna touch a penny," protested Para Handy, "if it wass not for my vessel's reputation; she needs a punt to give her an appearance."

A few days later the *Vital Spark* came into Tighnabruaich, and the Captain, by apparent accident, fell into converse with a hirer of rowing-boats.

"Man, you must be coinin' money," he said innocently; "you have a lot of boats."

"Coinin' money!" growled the boat-hirer; "no' wi' weather like this. I micht be makin' mair at hirin' umbrellas."

"Dear me!" said the Captain sympathetically, "that's a peety. A tidy lot o' boats, the most o' them; it's a wonder you would keep so many, and tred so bad."

"You werena thinkin' maybe o' buyin', were ye?" asked the boat-hirer suspiciously, with a look at the stern of the *Vital Spark*, where the absence of a punt was manifest.

"No," said the Captain blandly, "boats iss a luxury them days; they're lucky that doesna need them. Terrible weather! And it's goin' to be a dirty summer; there's a man yonder in America that prophesies we'll have rain even-on till Martinmas. Rowin'-boats iss goin' chape at Millport."

"If that's the look-out, they'll be goin' chape everywhere," incautiously remarked the boat-hirer.

"Chust that," said Para Handy, and made as if to move away. Then he stopped, and, with his hands in his pockets, pointed with a contemptuous foot at a dinghy he had had an eye on from the start of the conversation. "There's wan I aalways wondered at you keepin', Dan," said he; "she's a prutty old stager, I'll be bound you."

"That!" exclaimed the boat-hirer. "That's the tidiest boat on the shore; she's a genuine Erchie Smith."

"Iss she, iss she?" said the Captain. "I mind her the year o' the Jubilee; it's wonderful the way they hold thegither. A bad crack in her bottom strake; you wouldna be askin' much for her if a buyer wass here wi' ready money?"

"Are ye wantin' a boat?" asked the boat-hirer curtly, coming to the point.

"Not what you would caal exactly," said the Captain, "but if she's in the market I might maybe hear aboot a customer. What did you say wass the figure?"

"Three pound ten, and a thief's bargain," said the boat-hirer promptly, and Para Handy dropped at his feet the pipe he was filling.

"Excuse me startin'!" he remarked sarcastically, "you gave me a fright. It wass not about a schooner yat I was inquiring."

"She's worth every penny o't, and a guid deal mair," said the boat-hirer, and Para Handy lit his pipe deliberately and changed the subject.

"There's a great run on them motors," he remarked, indicating one of the launches in the bay. "My friend that iss wantin' a boat iss —"

"I thocht ye said ye werena wantin' ony kind o' boat at a',"
interjected the boat-hirer.

"Chust that; but there wass a chentleman that spoke to me aboot
a notion he had for a smaal boat; he will likely take a motor wan;
they're aal the go. That swuft! They're tellin' me they're doin' aal
the hirin' tred in Ro'sa' and Dunoon; there'll soon no' be a
rowin'-boat left. If I wass you I would clear oot aal the trash and
start a wheen o' motors."

"A motor wad be nae use for the *Vital Spark,*" said the boat-hirer,
who had no doubt now he had met a buyer. "Hoo much are ye
prepared to offer?"

"What for?" said Para Handy innocently, spitting on the desirable dinghy, and then apologetically wiping it with his hand.

"For this boat. Say three pounds. It's a bargain."

"Oh, for this wan! I wouldna hurt your feelings, but if I wass
wantin' a boat I wouldna take this wan in a gift. Still and on, a
boat iss a handy thing for them that needs it; I'm not denyin' it.
I'll mention it to the other chentleman."

"Wha is he?" asked the boat-hirer, and Para Handy screwed up
his eyes, and was rapt in admiration of the scenery of the Kyles.

"What you don't know you don't ken," he replied mysteriously.

"Ye couldna get a better punt for the money if ye searched the
Clyde," said the boat-hirer.

"I'm no' in any hurry; I'll take a look aboot for something aboot
two pound ten," said Para Handy. "Ye canna get a first-class boat
a penny cheaper. I got the offer of a topper for the forty shillings,
and I'm consuderin' it." He had now thrown off all disguise, and
come out in the open frankly as a buyer.

"Ye shouldna consider ower lang, then," said the boat-hirer;
"there's a lot o' men in the market the noo for handy boats o' this
cless; I have an offer mysel' o' two pounds fifteen for this very boat
no later gone than yesterday, and I'm hangin' oot for the three
pounds. I believe I'll get it; he's comin' back this afternoon."

"Chust that!" said Para Handy, winking to himself. "I'm sure
and I wish him weel wi' his bargain. She looks as if she would be
terrible cogly."

"Is Tighnabruaich quay cogly?" asked the boat-hirer indignantly. "Ye couldna put her over if ye tried."

"And they tell me she has a rowth," continued Para Handy,
meaning thereby a bias under oars.

"They're bars, then," said the boat-hirer; "I'll sell ye her for two
pound twelve to prove it."

The Captain buttoned up his jacket, and said it was time he was back to business.

"A fine boat," pleaded the boat-hirer. "Two pairs o' oars, a pair o' galvanised rowlocks, a bailin' dish, and a painter — dirt chape! take it or leave it."

"Would you no' be chenerous and throw in the plug?" said the Captain, with his finest irony.

"I'll dae better than that," said the boat-hirer. "I'll fling in a nice bit hand-line."

"For two pound ten, I think you said."

"Twa pound twelve," corrected the boat-hirer. "Come now, don't be stickin'."

"At two pounds twelve I'll have to consult my frien' the chentleman I mentioned," said the Captain; "and I'll no' be able to let you know for a week or two. At two pounds ten I would risk it, and it's chust the money I have on me."

"Done, then!" said the boat-hirer. "The boat's yours," and they went to the hotel to seal the bargain.

The boat-hirer was going home with his money when he heard the Captain stumping hurriedly after. "Stop a meenute, Dan," he said; "I forgot to ask if you haven't a bit of a net you might throw in, chust for the sake o' frien'ship?"

The boat-hirer confessed to his wife that he had made ten shillings profit on the sale of a boat he had bought for forty shillings and had three seasons out of.

Para Handy swopped the dinghy a fortnight later in Tarbert for a punt that suited the *Vital Spark* much better, and thirty shillings cash. With part of the thirty shillings he has bought another net. For flounders.

Chapter XIII

THE STOWAWAY

"*D*id you ever, ever, in your born days, see such umpidence?" said the mate of the smartest boat in the coasting trade, looking up from his perusal of a scrap of newspaper in which the morning's kippers had been brought aboard by Sunny Jim.

"What iss't, Dougald?" asked the Captain, sitting down on a keg to put on his carpet slippers, a sign that the day of toil on deck officially was over. "You'll hurt your eyes, there, studyin' in the dark. You're gettin' chust ass bad ass the enchineer for readin'; we'll have to put in the electric light for you."

"Chermans!" said Dougie. "The country's crooded wi' them. They're goin' aboot disguised ass towerists, drawin' plans o' forts and brudges."

"Now, isn't that most desperate!" said Para Handy, poking up the fo'c'sle stove, by whose light his mate had been reading this disquieting intelligence. "That's the way that British tred iss ruined. First it wass Cherman clocks, and then it wass jumpin'-jecks, and noo it's picture post-cairds."

"Criftens!" said Sunny Jim, who had come hurriedly down to put on a second waistcoat, for the night was cold: "Whit dae ye think they're makin' the drawin's for?"

"Iss't no' for post-cairds?" asked the Captain innocently, and the cook uproariously laughed.

"Post-cairds my auntie!" he vulgarly exclaimed. "It's for the German Airmy. As soon's they can get their bits o' things thegither, they're comin' ower here to fight us afore the Boy Scouts gets ony bigger. They hae spies a' ower Britain makin' maps; I'll lay ye there's no' a beer-shop in the country that they havena dotted doon."

"Holy smoke!" said Para Handy.

He watched the very deliberate toilet of Sunny Jim with some impatience. "Who's supposed to be at the wheel at this parteecular meenute?" he asked, with apparent unconcern.

"Me," said Sunny Jim. "There's naething in sicht, and I left it a meenute just to put on this waistcoat. Ye're gettin' awfu' pernicketty wi' your wheel; it's no' the Lusitania."

"I'm no' findin' faault at aal, at aal, Jum, but I'm chust considerin'," said the Captain meekly. "Take your time. Don't hurry, Jum. Would you no' give your hands a wash and put on a collar? It's always nice to have a collar on and be looking spruce if you're drooned in a collusion. Give a kind of a roar when you get up on deck if you see we're runnin' into anything."

"Collusion!" said Sunny Jim contemptuously. "Wi' a' the speed this boat can dae, she couldna run into a pend close if it started rainin'," and he swung himself on deck.

"He hasna the least respect for the vessel," said the Captain sadly. "She might be a common gaabert for aal the pride that Jum hass in her."

The *Vital Spark* had left Loch Ranza an hour ago, and was puffing across the Sound of Bute for the Garroch Head on her way to Glasgow. A pitch-black night, not even a star to be seen, and Sunny Jim at the wheel had occasionally a feeling that the Cumbrae Light for which he steered was floating about in space, detached from everything like a fire-balloon that winked every thirty seconds at the sheer delight of being free. He whistled softly to himself, and still very cold, in spite of his second waistcoat, envied Macphail the engineer, whom he could see in the grateful warmth of the furnace-door reading a penny novelette. Except for the wheeze and hammer of the engine, the propeller's churning, and the wash of the calm sea at the snub nose of the vessel, the night was absolutely still.

The silence was broken suddenly by sounds of vituperation from the fo'c'sle: the angry voices of the Captain and the mate, and a moment later they were on deck pushing a figure aft in front of them. "Sling us up a lamp, Macphail, to see what iss't we have a haad o' here," said the Captain hurriedly, with a grasp on the stranger's coat-collar, and the engineer produced the light. It shone on a burly foreigner with coal-black hair, a bronze complexion, and a sack of onions to which he clung with desperate tenacity.

"Got him in Dougie's bunk, sound sleepin'," explained the Captain breathlessly, with the tone of an entomologist who has found a surprising moth. "I saw him dandering aboot Loch Ranza in the mornin'. A stowaway! He wants to steal a trip to Gleska."

"I'll bate ye he's gaun to the Scottish Exhibeetion," said Sunny Jim. "We'll be there in time, but his onions'll gang wrang on him afore we get to Bowlin'. Whit dae they ca' ye for your Christian name, M'Callum?"

"Onions," replied the stranger. "Cheap onions. No Ingles."

"Oh, comeaffit! comeaffit! We're no'such neds as to think that ony man could hae a Christian name like Onions," said Sunny Jim. "Try again, and tell us it's Clarence."

"And what iss't your wantin' on my boat?" asked Para Handy sternly.

The foreigner looked from one to the other of them with large pathetic eyes from under a broad Basque bonnet. "Onions. Cheap onions," he repeated, extracting a bunch of them hastily from the bag. "Two bob. Onions."

"Gie the chap a chance," said Sunny Jim ironically. "Maybe he gie'd his ticket up to the purser comin' in."

"He hasna a word o' English in his heid," said Dougie. "There's something at the bottom o't; stop you, and you'll see! It's no' for his health he's traivellin' aboot Arran wi' a bag o' onions, and hidin' himsel' on board a Christian boat. I'll wudger that he's Cherman."

"It's no a German kep he's wearin' onyway," said Macphail, with the confidence of a man who has traveled extensively and observed.

"That's a disguise," said Dougie, no less confidently. "You can see for yoursel' he hass even washed himsel'. Try him wi' a bit of the Cherman lingo, Macphail, and you'll see the start he'll get."

Macphail, whose boast had always been that he could converse with fluency in any language used in any port in either hemisphere, cleared his throat and hesitatingly said, "Parly voo Francis?"

"Onions. Cheap onions," agreeably replied the stranger.

"Francis! Francis! Parly voo?" repeated the engineer, testily and loudly, as if the man were deaf.

"Maybe his name's no' Francis," suggested Sunny Jim. "Try him wi' Will Helm, or Alphonso; there's lots o' them no' called Francis."

"He understands me fine, I can see by his eye," said the engineer, determined to preserve his reputation as a linguist. "But, man! he's cunnin'."

"It's the wrong shup he hass come to if he thinks he iss cunnin' enough for us!" said the Captain firmly. "It's the jyle in Greenock that we'll clap him in for breakin' on board of a well-known steamboat and spoilin' Dougald's bunk wi' onions."

The stowaway sat nonchalantly down on a bucket, produced a knife and a hunk of bread, and proceeded to make a meal of it with onions. Immediately the crew was constituted into a court-martial, and treated the presence of their captive as if he were a deaf-mute or a harmless species of gorilla.

"What wass I tellin' you. Captain, at the very meenute I saw his feet stickin' oot o' my bunk?" inquired the mate. "The country's overrun wi' Chermans. I wass readin' yonder that there's two hunder and fifty thousand o' them in Brutain."

"What a lot!" said Para Handy. "I never set eyes on wan o' them to my knowledge. What are they like, the silly duvvles?"

"They're chust like men that would be sellin' onions," said Dougie. "Lerge, big, heavy fellows like oor frien' here; and they never say nothing to nobody. You've seen hunders o' them though you maybe didna ken. They're Chermans that plays the bands on the river steamers."

"Are they? are they?" said Para Handy with surprise; "I always thought yon chaps wass riveters, or brassfeenishers, that chust made a chump on board the boat wi' their instruments when she wass passin' Yoker and the purser's back wass turned."

"Germans to a man!" said Sunny Jim. "There's no' a Scotchman among them; ye never saw yin o' them yet the worse o' drink."

"Ye needna tell me yon chaps playin' awa' on the steamers iss makin' maps," said Para Handy. "Their eyes iss aalways glued on their cornucopias."

"They're goin' aboot ports and forts and battleships drawin' plans," said the engineer. "Whit did the Royal Horse Artillery find the ither day at Portsmouth? Yin o' them crawlin' up a gun to mak' a drawin' o't, and they had to drag him oot by the feet."

"Chust that!" said Para Handy, regarding their captive with greater interest. "I can see mysel' noo; he looks desperate like a Cherman. Do you think he wass makin' plans o' the *Vital Spark?*"

"That's whit I was askin' him in German!" said Macphail, "and ye saw yersel's the suspicious way he never answered."

"Jum," said the Captain, taking the wheel himself, "away like a smert laad and make up a cup o' tea for the chap; it's maybe the last he'll ever get if we put him in the jyle in Greenock or in Gleska."

"Right-oh!" said Sunny Jim, gladly relinquishing the wheel. "Will I set the table oot in the fore saloon? Ye'll excuse us bein' short o' floral decorations, Francis? Is there onything special ye would like in the way o' black breid or horse-flesh, and I'll order't frae the steward?"

"Onions," said the stranger. The foreigner spent the night imprisoned in the hold with the hatches down, and wakened with

an excellent appetite for breakfast, while the vessel lay at a wharf
on the upper river.

"There's money in't; it's like a salvage," Dougie said to Para
Handy, as they hurried ashore for a policeman.

"I canna see't," said the Captain dubiously. "What's the good
o' a Cherman? If he wass a neegur bleck, you could sell him to the
shows for swallowin' swords, but I doot that this chap hassna got
the right agility."

"Stop, you!" said the mate with confidence. "The Government
iss desperate keen to get a haad o' them, and here's Mackay the
polisman."

"We have a kind o' a Cherman spy on board," he informed the
constable, who seemed quite uninterested.

"The Sanitary Department iss up in John Street," said the
constable. "It's not on my bate." But he consented to come to the
Vita! Spark and see her stowaway.

"Toots, man! he's no' a Cherman, and he's no' a spy," he
informed them at a glance.

"And what iss he then?" asked the Captain.

"I don't ken what he iss, but he's duvvelish like a man that
would be sellin' onions," said Mackay, and on his advice the
suspect was released.

It was somewhat later in the day that Dougie missed his silver
watch, which had been hanging in the fo'c'sle.

Chapter XIV

CONFIDENCE

*T*he Captain of the *Vital Spark* and his mate were solemnly
drinking beer in a Greenock public-house, clad in their best
shore-going togs, for it was Saturday. Another customer came in
– a bluff, high-colored, English-spoken individual with an enor-

mous watch-chain made of what appeared to be mainly golden nuggets in their natural state, and a ring with a diamond bulging out so far in it that he could hardly get his hand into his trousers pocket. He produced a wad of bank-notes, peeled one off, put it down on the counter with a slap, and demanded gin and ginger.

"A perfect chentleman!" said Para Handy to his mate in a whisper; "you can aalways tell them! He'll likely have a business somewhere."

The opulent gentleman took his glass of gin and ginger to a table and sat down, lit a cigar, and proceeded to make notes in a pocketbook.

"That's the worst of wealth," said Dougie philosophically; "you have to be aalways tottin' it up in case you forget you have it. Would you care for chust another, Peter? I think I have a shullin'."

Another customer came in — apparently a seaman, with a badge of a well-known shipping line on his cap. "Hello, bully boys!" he said heartily. "Gather around; there's a letter from home! What are we going to have? In with your pannikins, lively now; and give it a name," and he ordered glasses round, excluding the auriferous gentleman who was taking notes behind.

"Looks like a bloomin' Duke!" he remarked in an undertone to Para Handy. "One of them shipowners, likely; cracker-hash and dandy-funk for Jack, and chicken and champagne wine for Mister Bloomin' Owner! Ours is a dog's life, sonnies, but I don't care now, I'm home from Callao!"

"Had you a good trup?" asked Para Handy, with polite anxiety.

"Rotten!" said the seaman tersely. "What's your line? Longshore, eh?" and he scrutinised the crew of the *Vital Spark*.

"Chust that!" said Para Handy mildly. "Perusin' aboot the Clyde wi' coals and doin' the best we can."

"Then I hope the hooker's your own, my boy, for there's not much bloomin' money in it otherwise," said the seaman; and Para Handy, not for the first time, fell a victim to his vanity.

"Exactly," he said, with a pressure on the toe of Dougie's boot; "I'm captain and owner too; the smertest boat in the tred," and he jingled a little change he had in his pocket.

"My name's Tom Wilson," volunteered the seaman. "First mate of the Wallaby, with an extra master's papers, d — n your eyes! And I've got five-and-twenty bloomin' quids in my pocket this very moment; look at that!" He flourished a wad of notes that was almost as substantial as the one displayed a little before by the gentleman with the nugget watch-chain.

"It's a handy thing to have aboot ye," said Para Handy sagely, jingling his coppers eloquently. "But I aalways believe in gold mysel'; you're not so ready to lose it."

"I've noticed that mysel'," said Dougie solemnly.

Tom Wilson ordered another round, and produced a watch which he confidently assured them was the finest watch of its kind that money could buy. It had an alarm bell, and luminous paint on the hands and dial permitted you to see the time on the darkest night without a light.

"Well, well! issn't that cluver!" exclaimed Para Handy. "They'll be makin' them next to boil a cup o' tea. It would cost a lot o' money? I'm no' askin', mind you; I wass chust remarkin'."

"Look here!" cried Tom Wilson impulsively; "I'll give the bloomin' clock to the very first man who can guess what I paid for it."

"Excuse me, gentlemen," said the man with the nugget watch-chain, putting away his notebook and pencil. "I'd like to see that watch," and they joined him at the table, where he generously ordered another round. He gravely examined the watch, and guessed that it cost about twenty pounds.

"Yes, but you must mention the exact figure," said its owner.

"Well, I guess two-and-twenty sovereigns," said the other, and Tom Wilson hastily proceeded to divest himself of the chain to which it had been originally attached. "It's yours!" he said; "you've guessed it, and you may as well have the bloomin' chain as well. That's the sort of sunny boy I am!" and he beamed upon the company with the warmth of one whose chief delight in life was to go round distributing costly watches.

"Wass I not chust goin' to say twenty-two pounds!" said Para Handy with some chagrin.

"I knew it wass aboot that," said Dougie; "chenuine gold!"

The lucky winner of the watch laughed, put it into his pocket, and took out the wad of notes, from which he carefully counted out twenty-two pounds, which he thrust upon Tom Wilson.

"There you are!" he said; "I wouldn't take your watch for nothing, and it happens to be the very kind of watch I've been looking for."

"But you have only got my word for it. Mister, that it's worth that money," protested Mr. Wilson.

The stranger smiled. "My name's Denovan," he remarked; "I'm up here from Woolwich on behalf of the Admiralty to arrange for housin' the torpedo workers in first-rate cottage homes with small back gardens. What does the Lords o' the Admiralty say to me?

The Lords o' the Admiralty says to me, 'Mr. Denovan, you go and fix up them cottage homes, and treat the people of Greenock with confidence.' I'm a judge of men, I am, bein' what I am, and the principle I go on is to trust my fellow-men. If you say two-and-twenty pounds is the value of this watch, I say two-and-twenty it is, and there's an end of it!"

Mr. Wilson reluctantly put the notes in his pocket, with an expression of the highest admiration for Mr. Denovan's principles, and Para Handy experienced the moral stimulation of being in an atmosphere of exceptional integrity and unlimited wealth. "Any wan could see you were the perfect chentleman," he confessed to Mr. Denovan, ducking his head at him. "What way are they aal keepin' in Woolwich?"

"I took you for a bloomin' ship-owner at first," said Mr. Wilson. "I didn't think you had anything to do with the Admiralty."

"I'm its right-hand man," replied Mr. Denovan modestly. "If you're thinkin' of a nice cottage home round here with front plot and small back garden, I can put you in, as a friend, for one at less than half what anybody else would pay."

"I haven't any use for a bloomin' house unless there was a licence to it," said Mr. Wilson cheerfully.

Mr. Denovan looked at him critically. "I like the look of you," he remarked impressively. "I'm a judge of men, and just to back my own opinion of you, I'll put you down right off for the first of the Admiralty houses. You needn't take it; you could sell it at a profit of a hundred pounds tomorrow; I don't ask you to give me a single penny till you have made your profit," and Mr. Denovan, producing his pocketbook, made a careful note of the transaction lest he might forget it. "'Treat the people of Greenock with confidence,' says the Lords of the Admiralty to me; now, just to show my confidence in you, I'll hand you back your watch, and my own watch, and you can go away with them for twenty minutes."

"All right, then; just for a bloomin' lark," agreed Tom Wilson, and with both watches and the colossal nugget-chain, he disappeared out of the public-house.

"That's a fine, smart, honest-lookin', manly fellow!" remarked Mr. Denovan admiringly.

"Do you think he'll come back wi' the watches?" said Dougie dubiously.

"Of course he will," replied Mr. Denovan. "Trust men, and they'll trust you. I'll lay you a dollar he would come back if he had twenty watches and all my money as well."

This opinion was justified. Mr. Wilson returned in less than five minutes, and restored the watches to their owner.

"Well, I'm jeegered!" said Para Handy, and ordered another round out of admiration for such astounding honesty.

"Would you trust me?" Mr. Denovan now asked Tom Wilson. "I would," said the seaman heartily. "Look here; I've five-and-twenty bloomin' quid, and I'll let you go out and walk the length of the railway station with them."

"Done!" said Mr. Denovan, and possessed of Wilson's roll of notes, went out of the public-house.

"Peter," said Dougie to the Captain, "do you no' think one of us should go efter him chust in case there's a train for Gleska at the railway station?"

But Tom Wilson assured them he had the utmost confidence in Mr. Denovan, who was plainly a tip-top gentleman of unlimited financial resources, and his confidence was justified, for Mr. Denovan not only returned with the money, but insisted on adding a couple of pounds to it as a recognition of Mr. Wilson's sporting spirit.

"I suppose you Scotch chaps don't have any confidence?" said Mr. Denovan to the Captain.

"Any amount!" said Para Handy.

"Well, just to prove it," said Mr. Denovan, "would you be willin' to let our friend Wilson here, or me, go out with a five-pound note of yours?"

"I havena the five pounds here, but I have it in the boat," said the Captain. "If Dougie'll wait here, I'll go down for it. Stop you, Dougie, with the chentlemen."

Some hours later Dougie turned up on the *Vital Spark* to find the Captain in his bunk, and sound asleep.

"I thocht you were comin' wi' a five-pound note?" he remarked on wakening him. "The chentlemen waited, and better waited, yonder on you, and they werena pleased at aal, at aal. They said you surely hadna confidence."

"Dougie," said the Captain, "I have the greatest confidence, but I have the five pounds, too. And if you had any money in your pocket it's no' with Mr. Denovan I would leave you."

Chapter XV

THE GOAT

*P*ara Handy, having listened with amazement to the story of the Stepney battle read by the engineer, remarked, "If it wassna in print, Macphail, I wouldna believe it! They must be desperate powerful men, them Rooshian burgulars. Give us yon bit again aboot Sir Wunston Churchill."

"'The Right Honorable gentleman, at the close of the engagement, went up a close and shook 127 bullets out of his Astrakan coat,'" repeated Macphail, who always added a few picturesque details of his own invention to any newspaper narrative.

"It was 125 you said last time," Para Handy pointed out suspiciously.

"My mistake!" said Macphail frankly; "I thocht it was a five at first, but I see noo it's a seven. A couple o' bullets more or less if it's anyway over the hundred doesna make much odds on an Astrakan coat."

"Man, he must be a tough young fellow, Wunston!" said the Captain, genuinely admiring. "Them bullets give you an awfu' bang. But I think the London polisman iss greatly wantin' in agility; they would be none the worse o' a lesson from Wully Crawford, him that wass the polisman in Tarbert when I wass at the school. Wully wouldna throw chuckles at the window to waken up the Rooshians; he wass far too caautious. He would pause and consuder. Wully wass never frightened for a bad man in a hoose: 'It's when they're goin' lowse aboot the town they're dangerous,' he would say; 'they're chust ass safe in there ass in my lock-up, and they're no' so weel attended.'

"Wully wass the first polisman ever they had in Tarbert. He wassna like the chob at aal, at aal, but they couldna get another man to take it. He wass a wee small man wi' a heid like a butter-firkin, full to the eyes wi' natural agility, and when he would put the snitchers on you, you would think it wass a shillin' he wass slippin' in your hand. If you were up to any muschief — poachin' a bit o' fish or makin' a demonstration — Wully would come up wi' his heid to the side and rubbing his hands thegither, and say a kindly word. I've seen great big massive fellows walkin' doon the street wi' Wully, thinkin' they were goin' to a Christmas pairty, and before they knew where they were they were lyin' on a plank in his lock-up. You never saw a man wi' nicer mainners; he wass the perfect chentleman!

"'Stop you there, lads, and I'll be back in a meenute wi' a cup o' tea,' he would say when he wass lockin' the door of the cell on them. 'Iss there anything you would like to't?' The silly idiots sometimes thocht they were in a temperance hotel by Wully's mainners, and they got a terrible start in the mornin' when they found they had to pay a fine. You mind o' Wully Crawfbrd, Dougie?"

"Fine!" said Dougie. "He was the duvvle's own!"

"'Caaution and consuderation iss the chief planks in the armor of the Brutish constable,' Wully used to say, rubbin' his hands. 'There iss no need for anybody to be hurt.'

"It wass the time when Tarbert herrin'-trawlers wass at their best and money goin'. It wass then, my laads, there wass Life in Tarbert! The whole o' Scotland Yaird and a regiment o' arteelery couldna have kept the Tarbert fishermen in order, but Wully Crawford held them in the hollow o' his hand —"

"It's a' very weel," said Macphail, "but they didna go aboot wi' automatic pistols."

"No, they didna have aromatic pistols," admitted Para Handy, "but they had aawfully aromatic fists. And you never saw smerter chaps wi' a foot-spar or a boat-hook. The wildest of the lot wass a lad M'Vicar, that belonged to Tarbert and wass called The Goat for his sagacity. He could punch his heid through a millstone and wear it round his neck the rest o' the day instead o' a collar. When The Goat wass extra lucky at the trawlin' the Tarbert merchants didna take the shutters off their shops and the steamboat agents had to put a ton or two o' ballast in their shippin'-boxes. Not a bad chap at aal. The Goat — only wicked, wicked! The only wan that could stand up to him in Tarbert wass three Macdougall brothers wi' a skiff from Minard; him and them wass at variance.

"The Goat would be going through the toun wi' his gallowses ootside his guernsey and his bonnet on three hairs, spreading devastation, when the Free Church munister would send for Wully Crawford.

"'You must do your duty, Wullium,' he would say, wi' his heid stickin' oot at a garret window and the front door barred. 'There's M'Vicar lowse again, and the whole o' Tarbert in commotion. Take care that ye divna hurt him.'

"'There's nobody needs to be hurt at aal, wi' a little deliberation,' Wully would say wi' his heid to the side, and it most dreadful like a butter-firkin. 'I'll chust paause and consuder, Mr. Cameron, and M'Vicar'll be in the cell in twenty meenutes. Terrible stormy weather, Mr. Cameron. What way's the mustress keepin'?'

"Then Wully would put off his uniform coat and on wi' a wee pea-jecket, and go up to where The Goat wass roarin' like a bull in the streets of Tarbert, swingin' a top-boot full o' stones aboot his heid — clean daft wi' fair defiance.

"'John,' Wully would say to him, rubbin' his hands and lookin' kindly at him, 'it's a wonder to me you would be carryin' on here, and them Macdougalls up on the quay swearin' they'll knock the heid off you.'

"The Goat would start for the quay, but Wully wass there before him, and would say to the Macdougalls, 'In to your boat, my laads, and on wi' the hatch; M'Vicar's vowing vengeance on you. Here he comes!' He knew very well it wass the last thing they would do; five minutes later and the three Macdougalls and The Goat would be in grips.

"'Pick oot whatever bits belong to yoursel's, and I'll collect what's left of poor M'Vicar,' Wully would say to the Macdougalls when the fight wass done, and then he would hurl The Goat to the lock-up in a barrow.

"But that wass only wan of Wully's schemes; his agility was sublime! There wass wan time yonder when The Goat took a fancy for high jeenks, and carried a smaal-boat up from the shore at night and threw it into the banker's lobby. It wass a way they had in Tarbert at the time o' celebratin' Hallowe'en, for they were gettin' splendid fishin's, and were up to aal diversions.

"Wully went roond in the mornin' to M'Vicar's house, and ass sure ass daith he hadna the weight or body o' a string o' fish, but a heid on him like a firkin. If The Goat had kent what he came for, he would have heaved him through the window.

"'You werena quarrelin' wi' Mackerracher last night and threw him ower the quay?' asked Wully, rubbin' his hands.

"I never set eyes on Mackerracher in the last fortnight!' said The Goat, puttin' doon a potato-beetle, as you might say disappointed.

"'Tuts! wassn't I sure of it!' said Wully, clappin' him on the back. 'Mackerracher's missin', and there's a man at the office yonder says he thocht he saw you wi' him. It's chust a case of alibi; come awa' across to the office for a meenute; he's waitin' there, and he'll see his mistake at wance.'

"The Goat went over quite joco to the polis-office, knowin' himsel' he wass innocent of any herm to poor Mackerracher, and wass fined in thirty shullin's for puttin' a boat in the banker's lobby. Oh, a cluver fellow, Wullium! A heid like a butter-firkin!

"You would think The Goat would never be got to the polis-office anymore wi' such contrivances o' Wully Crawford. 'If that wee duvvle wants me again, he'll have to come for me wi' the Princess Louisa's Own Argyll and Sutherland Highlanders and a timber-junker,' he swore, and Wully only laughed when he heard it. 'Us constables would be havin' a sorry time wi' the like of John M'Vicar if we hadna the Laaw o' the Land and oor wuts at the back o' us,' he said, wi' his heid on the side, and his belt a couple o' feet too big for him.

"Two or three weeks efter that, when the fishin' wass splendid, and The Goat in finest trum, he wakened one morning in his boat and found that someone had taken away a couple o' barrels o' nets, a pair o' oars, and a good pump-handle on him.

"'I'll have the Laaw on them, whoever it wass!' he says. 'Tarbert will soon be a place where a dacent man canna leave his boat withoot a watchdog; where's Wully Crawford, the polisman?"

"He went lookin' up and doon the toon for Wully, but Wully wasna to be seen at aal, at aal, and some wan said he wass over at the polis-office. The Goat went over to the polis-office and chapped like a chentlemen at the door withoot a meenute's prevarication.

"'Some wan stole on me through the night, a couple o' barrel o' nets, a pair o' oars, and a good pump-handle, and I want you to do your duty!' says The Goat to the polis-constable, and the head of him chust desperate like a butter-firkin!

"'Did you lose them, John?' said Wully, rubbin' his hands. 'Man! I think I have a clue to the depridaation; I have some of the very articles you're lookin' for in here,' and he opened the cell door, and sure enough there was a couple o' barrels o' nets in a corner. What did the silly idiot, John M'Vicar, no' do, but go into the cell to look at them, and the next meenute the door was locked on him!

"'A couple o' barrel o' nets and a pair o' oars or the like o' that can be taken in charge withoot assistance from the Princess Louisa's Own Argyll and Sutherland Highlanders,' said bold Wully through the keyhole. 'Iss there anything I could get for your breakfast tomorrow, John? You'll need to keep up your strength.

You're to be tried for yon assault last Saturday on the Rechabite Lodge.'

"The Goat lay in the cell aal day and roared like a bull, but it didna make any odds to Wully Crawford; he went aboot the toon wi' his heid more like a firkin than ever, and a kindly smile. But when The Goat begood at night to kick the door o' his cell for oors on end and shake the polis-office to its foundations, Wully couldna get his naitural sleep. He rose at last and went to the door o' the cell, and says, says he, 'John, ye didna leave oot your boots; if you'll hand them oot to me I'll gie them a brush for the mornin'.'

"M'Vicar put oot the boots like a lamb.

"'There now,' said Wully, lockin' the door again, 'ye can kick away till you're black in the face. Would you like them oiled or bleckened?' And you never saw a man wi' a heid more like a firkin o' Irish butter!"

Chapter XVI

PARA HANDY'S VOTE

*P*ara Handy had finished tea on Saturday night, and was ruefully contemplating the urgent need for his weekly shave, when Mary, his wife, was called to the outer door. She came back to the kitchen to inform her husband that a gentleman wished to see him.

"A chentleman!" said Para Handy, with surprise and even incredulity. "What in the world will he be wantin'?"

"He didna say," replied Mrs. Macfariane. "He said he wanted to see you most particular, and wouldna keep you a meenute. Whatever you do, don't go and buy another o' thae Histories of the Scottish Clans."

"Could you not tell him I'm away on the boat, or that I'm busy?" asked her husband, nervously putting on his jacket.

"I'm no' goin' to tell any lies aboot you," said Mrs. Macfarlane. "It's nobody for money anyway, for we're no' in anybody's reverence a single penny."

"What the duvvle can the man be wantin'? What kind o' look did you get at him? Do you think he's angry?"

"Not a bit of him; he spoke quite civil to mysel', and he has a book wi' a 'lastic band on't, the same as if it was the meter he was comin' for."

"A book!" said Para Handy, alarmed. "Go you out, Mary, like a cluver gyurl, and tell him that I slipped away to my bed when you werena lookin'. Tell him to come back on Monday."

"But you'll be away wi' the boat on Monday."

"Chust that; but he'll be none the wiser. There's many a sailor caaled away in a hurry. Don't be a frightened coward, Mary. Man, but you're tumid, tumid! The chentleman's no' goin' to eat you."

"He's no' goin' to eat you either," said Mrs. Macfarlane. "He's standin' there at the door, and you'll just have to go and see him."

"I wish I wass back on the boat," said Para Handy in despair. "There's no' much fun in a hoose o' your own if you'll no' get a meenute's peace in't. What in the mischief iss he wantin' wi' his book and his 'lastic bands?"

He went to the door and found an exceedingly suave young gentleman there, who said, "I'm delighted to find you at home. Captain Macfarlane; my business won't take five minutes."

"If it's a History o' the Clans, we have it already," said Para Handy, with his shoulder against the door. "I ken the clans by he'rt."

"You have a vote in the College Division," said the visitor briskly, paying no attention to the suggestion that he was a book-canvasser. "I'm canvassing for your old friend, tried and true, Harry Watt."

"Chust that!" said Para Handy. "What way iss he keepin', Harry? I hope he's in good trum?"

"Never was better, or more confident, but he looks to you to do your best for him on this occasion."

"That's nice," said Para Handy. "It's a blessin' the health; and there's lots o' trouble goin' aboot. Watch your feet on the stair goin' down; there's a nesty dark bit at the bottom landin'."

"Mr. Watt will be delighted to know that he can depend on you," said the canvasser, opening up his book and preparing to record one more adherent to the glorious principles of Reform. "He'll be sure to come round and give you a call himself."

"Anytime on Monday," said Para Handy. "I'll be prood to see him. What did you say again the chentleman's name wass?"

"Mr. Harry Watt," said the canvasser, no way surprised to find that the voter was in ignorance on this point, an absolute indifference to the identity of its M.P.s being not unusual in the College Division.

"Yes, yes, of course; I mind now. Harry Watt. A fine chentleman. Tip-top! He wass aalways for the workin' man. It's a fine open wunter we're havin' this wunter, if it wassna for the fogs."

"What do you think of the House of Lords now?" asked the canvasser, desirous to find exactly what his victim's color was, and Para Handy shifted his weight on another leg and scratched his ear.

"It's still to the fore," he answered cautiously. "There's a lot of fine big chentlemen in it. Me bein' on the boat, I don't see much of them, except noo and then their pictures in the papers. Iss there any Bills goin' on the noo?"

"I think we're going to clip their wings this time," said the canvasser with emphasis; and the Captain shifted hurriedly back to his former leg and scratched his other ear.

"Capital!" he exclaimed, apparently with the utmost sympathy. "Ye canna clup them quick enough. They're playin' the very muschief over yonder in Ireland. There's wan thing, certain sure — I never could stand the Irish."

"Yes, yes; but you'll admit a safe measure of Home Rule —" began the canvasser; and the Captain found the other leg was the better one after all.

"I'll admit that!" he agreed hurriedly. "Whatever you say yoursel'."

"See and be round at the poll early," said the canvasser. "It's on Thursday."

"I'm making aal arrangements," said the Captain cordially. "Never mind aboot a motorcar; I can walk the distance. Give my best respects to Mr. Harry; tell him I'll stand firm. A Macfarlane never flinched! He's no' in the shippin' line, Mr. Harry, iss he? No? chust that! I wass only askin' for curiosity. A brulliant chentleman! He hass the wonderful agility, they tell me. Us workin' men must stand thegither and aye be bringin' in a bill."

"Of course the question before the electors is the Veto," said the canvasser.

"You never said a truer word!" said the Captain heartily. "It's what I said mysel' years ago; if my mate Dougie wass here he would tell you. Everything's goin' up in price, even the very blecknin'."

"See and not be carried away by any of their Referendum arguments," counseled the canvasser, slipping the elastic band on his book. "It's only a red herring dragged across the track."

"I never could stand red herring," said the Captain.

"And remember Thursday, early — the earlier the better!" was the visitor's final word as he went downstairs.

"I'm chust goin' in this very meenute to make a note of it in case I should forget," said Para Handy, ducking his head reassuringly at him.

"A smert young fellow!" he told his wife when he got back to the kitchen. "He took my name doon yonder chust as nate's you like!" and he explained the object of the caller's visit.

"It's the like o' me that should have the vote," said Mrs. Macfarlane humorously. "I have a better heid for politics than you."

"Mery," said her husband warmly, "you're taalkin' like wan of them unfidel Suffragettes. If I see you goin' oot wi' a flag and standin' on a lorry, there'll be trouble in the College Diveesion!"

The Captain had hardly started to his shaving when Mrs. Macfarlane found herself called to the door again, and returned with the annoying intelligence that another gentleman desired a moment's interview.

"Holy smoke!" said Para Handy. "Do they think this hoose iss the Argyle Arcade? It must be an aawful wet night outside when they're aal crowdin' here for shelter. Could you no' tell him to leave his name and address and say I would caal on him mysel' on Monday?"

On going to the door he found an even more insinuative canvasser than the first one — a gentleman who shook him by the hand several times during the interview, and even went the length of addressing him like an old friend as Peter.

"I'm lucky to find you at home," he said.

"You are that!" said the Captain curtly, with his shoulder against the door. "What iss't?"

"I'm canvassing for our friend —"

"It's no' ten meenutes since another wan wass here afore," broke in the Captain. "You should take stair aboot, the way they lift the tickets in the trains, and no' be comin' twice to the same door. I made aal arrangements for the Thursday wi' the other chap."

"Think it over again," said the canvasser, no way crestfallen, with an affectionate hand on the Captain's shoulder. "Don't be misled by plausible stories. I have your name down here since last election as a staunch upholder of the Constitution. You must support Carr-Glyn."

"There's not a man in Gleska stauncher than mysel'," said the Captain. "What did you say the ohentleman's name wass?"

"Mr. Carr-Glyn," said the canvasser. "One of the good old sort; one of ourselves, as you might say; a nephew of the Duke of Argyll's."

"The very man for the job! I'll be there on Thursday; keep your mind easy on that. My mother wass a Campbell. The Duke iss a splendid chentleman. Tremendous agility!"

"The whole situation has changed in the last few days. You see, the Referendum practically puts the final decision upon every new constitutional change in the hands of the individual elector, and the Lords are gone."

"Cot bless me! you don't say so?" said the Captain with genuine surprise. "Where are they away to?"

The canvasser rapidly sketched the decline and fall of the hereditary principle in the Upper House.

"Holy smoke! iss the Duke goin' to lose his job, then?" asked Para Handy with sincere alarm; and the visitor hastened to reassure him.

"If you like, I'll send round a motorcar on Thursday," said the canvasser, when he had satisfied himself that the vote of Para Handy was likely to go to the side which had his ear last.

"Don't put yoursel' to any bother aboot a car; I would sooner walk: it's the least a body could do for Mr. Glyn," said the Captain. "Tell him that I'll stand firm, and that I'm terrible weel acquainted wi' his uncle."

"Thank you," said the canvasser. "Mr. Carr-Glyn will be highly pleased."

"You'll not answer the door the night again if a hundred chentlemen comes to it," said Para Handy when he got back to his wife. "A man might ass weel be livin' in a restaurant."

"What day's the pollin' on?" said Mary.

"On Thursday," said her husband. "Thank Cot! I'll no' be within a hundred miles o't. I'll be on the *Fital Spark* in Tobermory."

THE END

Lightning Source UK Ltd.
Milton Keynes UK
UKOW04f1606150817
307328UK00015B/145/P